DESIRE AND THE DEEP BLUE SEA

OLIVIA DADE

ISBN: 978-1-945836-05-3

ABOUT DESIRE AND THE DEEP BLUE SEA

They're pretending. Until they aren't.

Thomas McKinney has never wanted a woman the way he wants Callie Adesso. Since she started working alongside him at the Colonial Marysburg Research Library, he's spent his desk shifts fumbling pencils, tripping over his own feet, and struggling to remember both the Dewey Decimal System and the existence of her inconvenient boyfriend. Now, however, Callie is suddenly single—and in need of a last-minute faux-boyfriend for an episode of HATV's *Island Match*. Thomas is more than happy to play the part...and in the process, convince Callie that a week together isn't nearly long enough.

Callie has never found a man as irritating as she finds Thomas. He may be brilliant, kind, and frustratingly hand-some, but the absent-minded librarian also makes every workday an anxiety-inducing exercise in stress. Even seven days in paradise by his side won't change her opinion of him. Really. No matter how attentive he is. And gentle. And sexy.

One plane ride later, the two of them are spending long, hot days under the sun and on display, pretending to be in love for a television show. This may be a vacation, but it's also an act—as well as Thomas's last chance to persuade the woman of his dreams to include him in hers. And soon, the island heat isn't the only thing steaming up HATV's cameras...

PRAISE FOR OLIVIA DADE

With richly drawn characters you'll love to root for, Olivia Dade's books are a gem of the genre—full of humor, heart, and heat.

KATE CLAYBORN

Desire and the Deep Blue Sea was a delight of a novella. I gobbled it up in one bite and have no regrets. The hero is a swoon-worthy, bumbling academic, all cautious restraint and patient devotion. The heroine is an anxious badass (yes, those qualities can and usually do coexist), not to mention incredibly relatable. This book is pure catnip. Enjoy.

TALIA HIBBERT

For everyone who—like me—worries. Like, all the time. May you find love you never have to question or doubt.

ONE

CALLIE STARED DOWN AT HER DUMBPHONE WITH even more loathing than usual.

It couldn't connect to the internet, of course, but that wasn't why she hated it. God knew, she didn't need constant reminders via e-mail and social media notifications of everything she should worry about, not when some days she was already worried from the moment she woke up in the morning to the moment she made herself quit reading and turn off her bedside light. The cell's limited functionality was a feature, not a bug.

No, she hated her phone because she hated making calls and sending texts. Period.

And above all else, she hated it because she didn't want to make this particular call.

Just last month, she'd been given the numbers for Irene and Cowan, her intern contacts at Home and Away Television. Irene was kind of scary, to be honest. Cowan, though, had always seemed kind and reasonable, a model representative of America's most popular cable channel devoted to all matters home- and travel-related.

He'd also proven much less likely than Irene to sigh loudly whenever Callie took too long to respond to questions.

She needed patience and understanding right now, so she was calling Cowan. Maybe he could figure a way out of this mess for her, a path that would allow her to film her episode of HATV's *Island Match* without a boyfriend.

Even though that would violate the entire premise of the show.

Dammit. She didn't want to tap his name on her contacts list. But the breakroom door was closed, she was alone, and she couldn't delay any longer.

When he answered his cell, she used her Professional Librarian Voice. Tried to exude calm and competence and confidence in every syllable, despite her anxiety.

"Cowan? This is Callie Adesso. I think we may have a slight problem." She put the phone on speaker and laid it on the table in front of her, so she didn't have to hold it up with her trembling hand. "I wanted to let you know ASAP."

"Okay." His deep voice sounded cautious. "What's wrong?"

Before Callie could answer, she heard a distinctive and aggrieved female voice over the line. "Oh, Jesus, what now?"

Irene. Lord help them all.

"For God's sake, woman, you can't just snatch my—" Cowan made a sort of growly noise, and Callie could decipher the faint sounds of a scuffle. "My apologies, Callie. Hold on just a moment, please."

Everything went silent, as Callie blinked at her phone in befuddlement.

"We're back." Cowan sounded breathless. "And just so you know, you're on speaker phone so both Irene and I can hear what's going on. We're here to help. *Without any complaint.*"

Callie had a feeling that last bit wasn't directed at her.

A glance at the wall confirmed the sad truth. After dithering for so long, she only had ten minutes left of her break. She needed to get back on the desk with Thomas, much as she wished she didn't. There was no time to prevaricate or stall further.

"Andre and I broke up this morning," she told them. "He won't be able to film our episode of *Island Match* next week."

She could have sworn she heard Irene mutter *I told you so*.

"Callie..." Cowan's tone softened even further. "I'm so sorry. Are you okay?"

What would be the point of pretending? "Please don't worry. I'm not heartbroken."

Not about that, anyway.

Over the last couple of months, a relationship that had seemed promising if unspectacular had devolved into mutual dissatisfaction. Andre had stopped even pretending to listen to her, his bored gaze going unfocused whenever she tried to talk to him about her day or her worries or anything other than their dinner plans. And on the rare occasions he *did* pay attention to her, he'd begun responding to her concerns with increasing impatience. Telling her they were stupid and unfounded, and she just needed to get over them.

As if it were that easy. As if she hadn't already tried telling herself that thousands of times.

In return for his impatience, she'd begun responding to his amorous overtures with indifference. So she'd spent the last several weeks in a sexless, tension-filled relationship with a boyfriend whom she barely saw.

She should have ended things last month, probably. But starting a conversation about how and why their relationship had gone bad was way beyond her capabilities, as was a conversation about ending that relationship. If Andre hadn't broached the topic himself, she had no idea when it would have happened.

For someone like her, that kind of awkwardness and conflict could cause hives, and she wasn't inviting more Benadryl into her life.

So she'd stayed with Andre to avoid confrontation. Even more than that, though, she'd stayed with him for *Island Match*. For the beach.

Not Virginia Beach. Not even Myrtle Beach or Nags Head. After one too many jellyfish stings, she shied away from any body of water where she couldn't see her feet below the surface.

No, she needed clear Caribbean water. Sun-warmed sand beneath her soles. Lapping waves, their soothing rhythm carrying away her thoughts and leaving her brain in blissful peace.

And now she wasn't going to get any of it.

She blinked away the wetness blurring her vision.

"I'm glad you're not upset." Cowan sounded relieved not to have to comfort a grieving near-stranger over the phone. "Don't worry about the show. We'll take care of cancelling all the travel arrangements, including—"

His words failed to register as she swallowed a sob.

She'd considered the trip her reward. Not for earning her MLS and landing a good job at the Colonial Marysburg Research Library, or at least not entirely. Instead, for waging an endless war with her doubts and her frustrated loneliness at work. For the way she kept putting one foot in front of another and answering calls on the desk and helping patrons and pretending to be okay even when she wasn't, and the way she kept doing all of that until she *was* okay again.

In pursuit of that trip, she'd overcome her reluctance to be on TV. She'd convinced a resistant Andre to fill out the *Island Match* application. She'd filmed an interview alongside him. She'd talked on the phone countless time to Irene and Cowan, even when her library shifts had left her weary of people and conversation. She'd braced herself for limited cable-television fame and notoriety. She'd accepted the presence of new worries and uncertainty as the trip grew near.

Because she wanted that week on the beach. Needed it.

But she couldn't afford the trip on her own, not with her MLS-depleted savings, and she refused to ask for charity from her better paid and more successful family members.

So if she didn't speak now, she wouldn't go to a gorgeous Caribbean beach, not for months or years to come, and she'd never know what might have been. She'd always wonder whether she could have done something, said something, advocated for herself and gotten what she wanted.

God, speaking up was so hard.

Still, she was going to do it.

Maybe she could go on the trip by herself. Maybe she could substitute a friend or family member for Andre, and the show could proceed as normal. But she wouldn't know unless she asked.

"Cowan?" The word was thin and shaky. She could no longer summon Professional Librarian Voice. Instead, all she could muster was a frayed thread of sound.

Still, Cowan stopped talking immediately. "Yes?"

She squeezed her eyes closed and tried to breathe, but her brief, bright burst of conviction was already fading, even as a familiar fiery prickle spread across her chest.

Literally every episode of *Island Match* involved a romantic couple. No exceptions. Why would she think they'd alter the entire premise of the show just for her?

If she kept bothering them, Cowan and Irene were going to hate her, if they didn't already, for delaying the inevitable. For asking questions and causing them more effort and trouble instead of simply disappearing into the ether.

Besides, no one *owed* her a beach vacation. Someone else deserved this opportunity, and Cowan and Irene deserved to get off the phone so they could deal with the aftermath of Callie's problems.

She needed to keep her mouth shut. Avoid confrontation. Keep forcing a smile and wait until the pretense of being fine became reality.

Yes, speaking up was so hard.

Too hard for someone like her.

"I'm sorry," Callie whispered.

Cowan's voice was gentle. "It's okay." After a moment, he spoke again. "Like I said, you have nothing to worry about. We'll take care of all the cancellations on our end. Do you have any other questions?"

No. Everything seemed clear. Terrible, yes, but clear.

"I—" Callie gulped back another sob. "I don't—"

At that moment, when her personal history would have predicted that she would acquiesce to the inevitable, choke out a goodbye to Cowan and Irene, and never bother HATV again, a dark head of curls crowning a concerned face appeared through the little window in the breakroom door.

Thomas.

So tall. So handsome. So smart. So kind.

Such a pain in the ass.

He must be stooping, because otherwise she'd only see his chest in that square of glass.

His dark brows had furrowed above those ocean-blue eyes, and he made some sort of weird chin-jerk at her. Oddly enough, she could translate that gesture.

He'd heard something that worried him, even through the door. Which seemed impossible, given both the ambient noise in the library and the single-minded, damnable focus he normally displayed on the desk.

However improbably, though, he'd detected something

amiss. And now he wanted to know if she needed help. As if he, the architect of her current despair, the main reason she needed a freaking beach vacation to begin with, could solve her problems.

She sniffed back more tears and waved him away.

When he didn't budge, she waved him away again.

At that, he pressed his lips together, horizontal lines scored across his high forehead, and slowly, reluctantly, left the window.

She stared after him for a moment.

Single. Thomas was single. Charming in his own way. Exceedingly telegenic, she'd guess.

And she'd seen his upcoming schedule. As soon as the spreadsheet came out every month, she immediately compared her shifts to his. Out of morbid curiosity, of course, and also to confirm once again just how thoroughly she was fucked.

Their schedules were always in sync. Always. No matter how fervently she wished they weren't, or how late she entered her schedule requests. Somehow, even if she waited until the very last hour, his requests still came in after hers, and whatever he put would mean the two of them were on the desk at the same time.

It was inevitable. Unavoidable. Like choosing the slowest checkout lane at the grocery store.

This month was no different. They were working together almost every shift. And for some bizarre reason, he'd even taken vacation next week, the same week as her.

Maybe it was all a huge coincidence. Or maybe he knew her work ethic would allow him to function as he preferred on the desk—i.e., at the pace of a molasses-coated sloth—and he was gaming the system.

The latter possibility had caused her no small amount of rage over the past few months.

But before then, back when she'd first started at the library, she'd searched for his lean, handsome face in the breakroom and sighed happily when she'd found it. She'd arrived early at work to talk with him about whatever she was reading that day. She'd showed him pictures of her nieces and nephews, and he'd smiled down at the images with such gentleness she'd nearly gone liquid.

She didn't want to remember. It *hurt* to remember. But she couldn't seem to help herself.

And at that moment, something in her brain shorted out.

She cleared her throat. When she opened her mouth again, Professional Librarian Voice rang out, loud as her heartbeat and clear as the Caribbean.

"I do have another question, Cowan." Inexplicably, her mouth had said that. Her voice. "What would you say if I told you I had a new boyfriend?"

As soon as the last word emerged from her mouth, her face twisted into an instinctive wince, her stomach began to roil, and her skin might as well have burst into flame.

Oh, Jesus. What had she done?

She never spoke without thinking. Ever. So why had she done it now? To representatives of a cable television network, of all people? The two of them were in the entertainment industry, for God's sake. Savvier and way more sophisticated than a woman like her.

They *had* to know she was lying. But they weren't saying anything.

If they remained quiet much longer, Callie was going to throw up.

Confronted with such a brazen falsehood, maybe they'd lost the power of speech. Maybe they'd muted the phone or were communicating via carrier pigeon or semaphore flags about how much they hated her. Maybe they were preparing to hang up on her. She didn't know, and the uncertainty was killing her.

Finally, Irene broke the silence.

"My, my, my. Callie Adesso, total dark horse." For the first time in Callie's memory, the other woman sounded highly entertained. "Didn't you say you broke up with your ex earlier this morning?"

"Yes." Callie paused. "It was a long time coming."

"I'll bet," Irene said.

"But just to be clear," Callie rushed to add, "Thomas and I didn't get involved until after I was free."

She was already a liar. No need to make herself sound like a cheater too.

The other woman snorted. "You're telling me you didn't stray while you were with Andre, but you *did* find a new guy before lunchtime on the same day you became single? Is that right?"

Lying wasn't as easy or fun as she'd been led to believe.

"Umm…" Callie bit her lip. "Yes. That's right."

A gleeful laugh crackled through the cell's speaker. "I don't know whether to check your pants for flames or congratulate you for finally kicking that asshole to the curb."

At that, Callie's eyes widened. "You thought Andre was an assh—"

Cowan didn't let her finish. "I'm sorry, Callie. The timing of your relationships is none of our business. Also, HATV and its employees would never call one of our applicants an asshole. Ever. Not under any circumstances. Please excuse us for a moment."

They must have muted their conversation again, because she couldn't hear anything for a few seconds. By the time they returned, she was nibbling on a thumbnail, trying not to scratch her chest.

"Apologies for calling your ex an asshole." Irene didn't

sound especially sorry, and she didn't wait for her apology to be accepted. "We have a few more questions."

"Forgive us," Cowan said, "but how do we know this man is really your boyfriend?"

The true moment of decision had arrived. If she backed out now, Irene and Cowan wouldn't belabor the issue. They'd merely hang up and find someone else for the show.

But if she kept lying, she'd actually have to provide evidence of that lie.

She could either continue on the Dark Path of Duplicity, or she could make a sharp right onto the Rosy Roadway to Righteousness. And she had to make the choice now.

"Ummm…" She closed her eyes and grimaced. "After work tonight, I can e-mail you pictures of us together, and you can judge for yourself whether we look romantically involved. Or you can send someone to interview us, like you did with Andre."

Trundling along the Dark Path of Duplicity it was, then.

And somehow, she was still talking. "All this might seem a bit quick—"

"You think?" Irene said.

"—but Thomas and I have worked together for months now, and there've always been, uh, feelings." Irritation and impatience were feelings, right? "We just didn't act on them before this. Until Andre and I ended things."

Shit, shit, shit. How had the scope of this lie not occurred to her? Did she really plan to create fake pictures of them as a loving couple? Or convince Thomas to memorize and parrot a fictional story about their torrid love affair?

"We don't have time to do another interview before the trip." After a muffled conversation with Cowan, Irene came back on the line. "Tell us about your new boyfriend, Callie."

He makes a tortoise seem speedy. Fails to multitask or retain basic information about checkout procedures. Bumps into the microfilm machines and various desks while deep in thought.

No. That wouldn't do.

Instead of dwelling on her more recent frustrations, Callie conjured up her first impressions of Thomas, back when she'd found him charming. Sought out his company.

This part of the lie would be comparatively easy.

"His name is Thomas McKinney. He's thirty-five and unfairly handsome." Picturing him, every detail of that too-attractive face and long body, was easier than she'd like. "He has dark, curly hair with a little silver just starting at the temples. Pale skin. Eyes like…" She thought about it. "In the Caribbean, you know how the water close to shore is turquoise, but if you go out a bit further, it's ridiculously blue? That's his eye color."

Cowan made a weird choking sound. "Ridiculously blue?"

Engrossed in her description of Thomas, Callie barely heard the intern. "He's tall. Lean, but really strong. When we had to move our encyclopedia collection, he was able to carry these enormous stacks of books." Well, until he'd tripped over a cart and dumped various volumes all over the polished wooden floor. "Plus, patrons flirt with him all the time, and he doesn't seem to notice."

That obliviousness always made her feel just a tiny better during their shifts together.

"Maybe you could—" Cowan started to say.

"Sometimes he wears dark-rimmed glasses, and they suit him way too well. It's like he's a bookish spy or a really sexy professor, which can be very distracting." She hesitated. "Sorry. What were you saying?"

Irene blew out a loud breath. "Can you tell us something else about him? Something that doesn't involve how hot he is?"

Oh. She supposed she had kind of rambled about his

looks for a bit too long. Probably because she didn't have much practice with lying.

"He's very intelligent." Maybe the smartest man she'd ever met, but she would keep that little tidbit to herself. "He started at the library six months before I was hired, so he's been here a year. He has a Ph.D. in American history and knows a ton about different time periods."

"That's plenty of—"

Callie barely heard Cowan. "When he gets a tricky question on the desk, he'll do everything he can to answer it as thoroughly and accurately as possible, no matter how long it takes. He's dogged, he's curious, and he truly wants to help people."

All true. Cowan and Irene simply didn't need to know how all that endless patience and curiosity impacted Callie. How by the time she'd started working at the library, the researchers and interpreters with more interesting and complex questions had already learned to go to him for answers when he was on the desk. How she got stuck with all the basic factual and circulation questions, and her own knowledge of history and the library remained untapped. How she had to deal singlehandedly with any lines at the desk, because he would spend almost his entire shift on one or two people and fail to offer assistance when she was in the weeds. How she was continually forced to calm patrons who were frustrated at the wait for help. How she had to hurry through any interesting questions she *did* receive, because of that line and those pissed-off people in it.

Cowan and Irene didn't need to know that working with Thomas all the time had stopped Callie from forming closer ties with patrons and other colleagues and left her feeling increasingly isolated.

So instead, she tried to remember more of the good stuff.

The reasons she used to rush to work half an hour early so she and Thomas could hang out before her shift started.

"He's kind. Easy to talk to." Somehow, amidst her burgeoning anger and worry, she'd forgotten that. "Not particularly familiar with pop culture but interested in everything. And he has this wry sense of humor with absolutely no meanness to it. No mockery whatsoever."

At first, she'd chatted with him all the time, and he'd always listen intently to whatever she wanted to say. Then he'd ask her questions or offer up his own well-considered opinions with that quiet confidence she so envied, and they'd talk for hours in the parking lot after work. Those chats hadn't been mere water cooler talks or gossip sessions, but the sorts of conversations she'd always hoped to have with her boyf—

Nope. Not ambling down that particular mental road.

It didn't matter how good a conversationalist he was. As her aggravation with him had grown, she'd stopped talking to him unless work required it. Because having all his careful attention, all his decency and kindness, directed her way somehow felt even worse than if he'd been a dick.

If he'd been a dick, her anger wouldn't feel so petty. If he'd been a dick, she might have mustered the courage to complain, either to him or to a supervisor. But he was a good man. She didn't want to hurt his feelings, she didn't want to get him in trouble, and she didn't want to borrow conflict or seem high-maintenance at a place where she'd only worked for six months.

Just the thought of confronting him made her itch.

So she was stuck. Frustrated and lonely and sad, but silent.

Irene interrupted her thoughts. "I think we're good here."

"What…" Callie swallowed, too nervous to hope. "What does that mean?"

"It means you've convinced me. You're into this dude, no question about it. We can make this work."

Wow. She was an *excellent* liar. Who knew?

"Have him fill out the online application tonight. We'll do the interview and take some pictures when you arrive at the first island." Cowan sounded distracted, and Callie could hear a tapping sound, as if he were taking notes. "I'll update the tickets and reservations and send you all the confirmation messages as soon as I can."

Her eyes were swimming again, and she wiped them against the sleeve of her blouse.

She'd done it. Oh, God, she'd done it.

Next week, she'd be digging her toes into white sand and splashing in the surf, allowing the water to erode all her worries as she luxuriated in the best trip of her life.

That is, if she could convince Thomas to abandon his previous vacation plans, lie on cable television, and spend an entire week in close proximity with a coworker who hadn't talked to him for several months.

Oh, God, she *hadn't* done it. Not really. Not yet.

She didn't need to blink back happy tears anymore. Her eyes were as dry and gritty as that imaginary white sand. "Got it. Is there anything else I need to know?"

"One last thing." Cowan was silent for a moment. "I'm choosing to believe that you and Thomas McKinney are a couple, because I like you. And, to be frank, because cancelling your trip would mess up the entire *Island Match* schedule for the rest of the season. But there will be cameras on you almost constantly for days. If you're lying…"

When he paused again, she squeezed her eyes shut, shame suffusing her cheeks with heat.

Finally, he sighed. "If you're lying, Callie, do it well."

TWO

"So I told them you were my boyfriend." Callie fiddled with a strand of her dark hair, her face twisted into a grimace. "I'm sorry. I shouldn't have dragged you into my issues."

Thomas blinked at her, startled and somewhat confused, but not unhappy.

Nope. Not at all.

Callie and Andre had broken up. Finally. She'd said the split was a long time coming, and Thomas had to concur. To him, it had felt like centuries. Millennia.

Apparently, Thomas and Callie were also going to spend a week together in various tropical paradises. While being filmed, from what he understood. And while those weren't necessarily optimal circumstances for wooing such a mercurial woman, they were certainly better than reading in his condo while she cavorted on the beach with her ex.

As far as he knew, he hadn't tossed a coin into an enchanted well, procured a potion from a witch, or fondled a lamp of mysterious provenance. But he could think of no other plausible explanation for these miraculous turns of events, so maybe he'd missed something.

Most importantly, Callie had stopped crying, and that was enough to set his world aright once more. He could wait for clarity on everything else.

That said, he should probably determine a few key facts before they proceeded.

"Let me make sure I understand the situation." He leaned against his hybrid's sun-heated hood in the stifling humidity of the library lot. "Next week, we're flying to three islands for one night each. And then we'll choose one of those islands for the last three nights of our trip."

She nodded. "Whichever one is our favorite."

"And HATV will film us in the belief that we're a couple."

Her nod was a bit more tentative that time. "Yes."

"Did we…" He hated to ask. It made him sound like a dunce, and he didn't think even he could have missed such a crucial development. But he needed to know for sure. "Did we agree to date at some point?"

If so, he had no memory of it happening. And when Callie spoke to him, looked at him, or hell, just breathed in his general direction, she captured his full and utterly devoted attention in a way no other woman ever had.

So he'd probably remember if they'd talked about dating.

Callie was shaking her head so hard, she had to be giving herself a headache. "No. No. God, no. You were just nearby, single, and on vacation next week, so I thought you'd be a good candidate for the job."

Too bad. Learning that he'd won her affections while in a fugue state of some sort would have been convenient. But no matter. He had a week to do the job while completely conscious.

"Thomas…" She was nibbling on that plump lower lip, a signature gesture that had caused him to fumble various writing implements over the past six months. "I should've asked you before saying anything to them. But I just"—her inhalation turned shaky, her eyes shiny, and he would have torn apart the concrete parking lot with his bare hands to assuage her distress—"I just need this vacation. So badly. Can you possibly play along with me? Or did you already have plans? I know this was meant to be your summer break."

"I wasn't doing anything important." He shrugged. "I'd planned to read about the influenza pandemic during World War I, but that can wait."

Her eyes grew bright in a different, better way. "Last year, I read *The Great Influenza*, and I really appreciated Barry's discussion of—" She stopped herself. "Never mind. That's not the point right now. Are you really agreeing to go along with my stupid plan?"

"Not stupid." Reaching out, he touched her elbow. Just for a moment, through the silky barrier of her blouse, but the contact still dizzied him. "Ingenious, given the urgency of the situation. And yes, I'm agreeing to your plan."

Her lips parted, and she stared up at him for a moment. "I can't believe you said yes."

Any opportunity he could find to spend time with her, he'd take. Even if it meant relinquishing his favorite morning shifts to work in the afternoons and evenings. Even if it meant attending work gatherings at noisy, overcrowded bars. Even if it meant spending a week on camera and possibly making a fool of himself in front of a cable-television-viewing audience.

When Callie Adesso began working at the CMRL, the axis of his life shifted. From what he could tell, that shift appeared absolute and irrevocable.

And she'd been dating another man the entire time they'd known one another, until now.

If that relationship had been going awry for quite some time, as she'd said, maybe that would explain her seeming unhappiness the last few months. Because she didn't smile at him the same way she once did, and they didn't laugh and talk before or after their shifts anymore.

He hadn't understood it. But maybe this unexpected trip would explain everything.

Even better: Maybe this unexpected trip would *change* everything.

"Believe it," he told her.

"I FIRST MET CALLIE WHEN SHE BEGAN HER training at the library," he told the camerawoman-cum-interviewer. "Next Thursday, we will have known each other for precisely seven months."

Callie's gaze whipped to his. "That's…" She paused, and her lips moved as she did some mental math. "That's right."

For some reason, she sounded befuddled. Which befuddled him in turn, because how could he forget the day of her arrival at CMRL? How could anyone?

Maybe the preparations for the trip to Parrot Cay had tired her. He could understand that. His past several days had been a whirlwind of filling out applications and releases and waivers, followed by haphazard packing and emergency purchases of sunscreen and swim trunks. And despite all the hubbub, he'd still spent each night awake and wondering. Hoping.

Planning.

So he could empathize with any exhaustion she was experiencing. Although, to be fair, he'd never taken such a comfortable trip before, and he likely never would again.

First-class tickets didn't come cheaply enough for a man still paying off his student loans.

The seats had been wide and well-cushioned, the leg room generous, the movie choices endless. But the best part of the whole experience, by far: seeing Callie's face illuminate when the flight attendant had handed them menus, and she'd realized their tickets had bought them a three-course meal. A delicious one, at that.

"I love red snapper and plantains," she'd whispered to him, those coffee-brown eyes wide. "And I'm going to dive headfirst into the key lime mousse."

Scratch that. The best part of the journey was watching her take her first bite of that tart-sweet mousse, her eyes scrunched closed and her lips curved in pleasure.

Or possibly when she'd finished her second glass of champagne and giggled at him for the first time in months when he'd noted the inadvisability of reading a book about pandemics on an airplane.

Or maybe when, as they'd skipped over waves on the ferry ride to Parrot Cay, she'd managed to stop him from falling overboard by hauling his body against hers.

He'd been watching her, as usual, admiring how the sun limned strands of her wind-whipped hair with fire. In the midst of such intense concentration, though, he hadn't noticed the rather large swell approaching the small vessel or braced himself for the impact.

So she'd saved him. And for several glorious moments, he'd been pressed against her, face to face, her warmth to his heat. The softness of her breasts and belly fit into the contours of his body like connecting puzzle pieces. That glorious brown hair lashed against his face in the ocean breeze, the sting more than welcome. Her strong arms held him in a steady, firm grip. And her flowery fragrance surrounded him. Intoxicated him.

Then she'd let him go in a hurry, and he'd chosen to sit on the deck for the rest of the ferry ride instead of testing his overwhelmed senses further.

Upon their arrival at Parrot Cay, they'd been greeted at the dock by HATV crew members—including Gladys, their episode's producer—and ushered into a generic meeting room inside the private island's enormous, pristine hotel. The small crew had already prepared the room for the interview, setting two chairs cozily next to one another in front of the cameras and beneath the boom mic.

Callie was sitting mere centimeters away from him, her thigh warm beneath her gauzy skirt. And he knew the heat of that thigh intimately, since it was touching his. The scent of flowers had faded at some point. She now smelled like sunscreen and sweat, his new favorite fragrance.

All in all, this trip was already one of the highlights of his life, and they hadn't even posed for pictures as a couple yet. He had high hopes for the afternoon.

The camerawoman checked the next question on her list. "Tell us what first attracted you to Callie."

This interview was only supposed to take a few minutes, since they needed to check into their rooms and take a guided tour of the island before sunset. That question alone could occupy the rest of their time on Parrot Cay, however.

Where to start? And how to say it succinctly?

"Her face," he told the camerawoman, and then paused. "I noticed her face."

Apparently he'd been too succinct. Because after a moment of silence, Callie stifled another giggle, and Gladys rolled her eyes.

"Care to elaborate?" the camerawoman asked.

Well, if HATV wanted to know more, he was happy to tell them.

"First of all, she's obviously gorgeous." He swept a hand

in Callie's direction, vaguely aware that her giggles had come to an abrupt stop. "So of course I appreciated that. Anyone would."

He wouldn't expound on the lushness of her body to the world, because he didn't want to embarrass her. But only a fool would look at her ample curves—solidity and softness combined into a form that stopped his breath—and fail to appreciate that kind of beauty.

"But it's more than that. Her face…" He tried to put all he'd seen, all he'd worshipped, into words. "Her face changes. When she's happy, it's open and bright enough to blind me. When she's upset, everything shutters. And when she's angry, her brows lower, her eyes narrow, and she could stop the tides with a single look."

Those thick, dark brows of hers said everything. Everything.

"So her face is expressive," Gladys paraphrased.

He warmed to his favorite topic. "But it's not just her face that's mercurial. Depending on what she wears, she looks completely different from day to day. One shift, she might slick back her hair and wear dark red lipstick and leather boots and look ready to kick James Bond's ass. But the next day, her hair will be all bouncy and wavy, and she'll wear a flowery dress and something shiny on her lips, and if spring meadows needed to advertise, she would star in those advertisements."

Gladys's eyes had gone wide, but she wasn't interrupting him.

"Sometimes her hair seems almost black, and sometimes it's almost red. Her skin is pale in the winter but golden in the summer, even though I've seen her put on sunscreen. Her perfume changes too." He turned to Callie, who'd gone very still beside him. "Every day, from what I can tell. Is that right? Do you use a different perfume every day?"

Earlier today, she'd smelled heady, like late-summer blooms. Tomorrow, she might smell like berries or lemons or rosemary or musk. Ever-changing and ever-enticing.

He loved that about her.

"I…" She licked her lips, even though they were still shellacked with that shiny gloss he adored. "I like perfume samples."

That explained it.

"And she can do anything." He returned his attention to Gladys, eager for her to understand the full glory of the woman beside him. "Did you know she was working full-time as a costumed interpreter even as she took all the classes she needed for her master's degree? And no matter what people ask while she's on the desk, she can find the answer quickly. She picked up the circulation system in less than three days, she could locate any of our reference materials with her eyes closed, and she can chat with our patrons about anything. Television shows, movies, science, history, whatever. Because she's so damn intelligent and curious, and her mind works in a way mine doesn't."

He waved a hand dismissively. "I can't multitask to save my life, but she's good at everything. So good, I found it intimidating at first, but then I decided just to admire it. To watch her and enjoy the sight of someone who can do anything and be anyone she wants."

A gentle hand landed on his knee. Warm. Soft. Tipped with sparkly pink nails.

They'd been red only last week. She was a wonder.

"Thomas," Callie whispered. "I had no idea."

Those brown eyes of hers had gone sad, and he didn't understand it. Hadn't he expressed himself well enough?

He needed to wrap this up and figure out what he'd done wrong. "In summation, everything about her attracted me. She's energetic and witty and kind to everyone, unless they try to return books stained by cat urine. She's frighteningly intelligent and competent. And of course, she's obviously beautiful. So who wouldn't be attracted to her? There are probably people in the future desperately trying to invent time travel so they can come back to the twenty-first century and meet her."

When he finished, neither of the women said anything for a long, long time. But Callie hadn't moved her hand from his knee, and he felt that light touch like a brand.

"Wellllll..." Gladys drew out the word, her gray brows near her hairline. "I think that pretty much covers the question."

"Can we—" Callie swallowed, then started again. "Can we maybe check in and take our tour first, and then finish the interview later? I think I need a few minutes."

He stood immediately. Loath to lose her hand, though, he laced his fingers through hers and helped her to her feet. "If Callie's tired, we should take a break. Let's go find our room."

In the cool privacy of their own space, he'd try to determine what emotions kept chasing each other across her expressive face, appearing and vanishing too quickly for him to decipher them. And then he'd put his plan into action.

He might not be able to multitask. He might not understand popular culture.

But he knew how to train his absolute focus on a question and find an answer. He knew how to consider a single subject and explore it top to bottom, inside and out. He knew how to research, and he knew how to gather his data and create a persuasive argument.

By the end of this week, he'd have an answer to the question of whether Callie might ever grow to love him the way he did her. And if that was even a distant possibility, he would compile his data and prepare his arguments and present his thesis to her before their return to Marysburg.

His thesis statement was simple, but it was powerful. Just five short words.

I could make you happy.

THREE

"CALLIE, PLACE YOUR HANDS ON THOMAS'S LEFT shoulder, one stacked on top of the other," Gladys instructed. "Now look up at him."

Callie obeyed, her chest oddly tight.

Thomas's shoulder muscles bunched at the first touch of her fingers, and when he turned his head and gazed down at her, she could have sworn he didn't see or hear anyone else on the planet. He covered both her hands with one of his, his smile sweet and soft and meant only for her, cameras or no cameras.

Those long, lean hands could heft a mountain of encyclopedias.

But he touched her as if she were a priceless piece of eighteenth-century Delftware.

He tilted his head forward, until he encompassed her world. "Everything okay?"

"Fine," she whispered back, and he nodded, but he didn't look convinced.

He'd asked the same question when they'd checked into their lavish suite, which—to her mingled horror and excitement—contained only one bed. One enormous, fluffy-looking bed. But she hadn't answered him then. Instead, she'd merely told him they needed to take photos before their tour of the island. Which was true, but also a way to buy herself time to think.

"Now put both arms around his waist and smile, Callie. Thomas, bend your neck and rest your forehead against hers." Gladys waited for them to follow directions, then tsked in disapproval. "Tighter, please. You should be pressed right up against one another."

If she moved any closer, even by a millimeter, she might spontaneously combust. And she couldn't decide whether the prospect of burning to ash in Thomas's arms sounded more frightening or irresistible.

So instead of shifting, she stayed completely still.

Thomas studied her face for a long moment, and then flicked a glance at Gladys. "Just a moment, please."

Ducking his head, he murmured in Callie's ear, "I don't want to do anything that makes you uncomfortable. Just say the word, and I'll make up some excuse why a certain pose doesn't work for me. Or you can pinch my arm. Or *something*."

Sincerity and concern fairly glowed from every line of his face, even as unmistakable heat poured from that long, lean body of his. Even as she stepped closer, and his eyes went heavy-lidded. Even as his fingertips on the flesh of her back tightened and trembled, biting pleasurably through her blouse before loosening once more.

"Don't worry," she told him.

He didn't appear satisfied with that answer. "I mean it, Callie."

"I know."

She couldn't help smiling at him, just as Gladys had

requested. And when she did, he blinked a few times. As if she really had blinded him.

Maybe she'd been confused up in their suite, but given a few minutes to think, given a few minutes to feel how he touched her, Callie could only reach one conclusion.

Unless Thomas planned to make his big-screen debut in the immediate future, he wasn't play-acting for the cameras when he held her hand, looked at her with tender affection in those blue, blue eyes, or expounded on what he—bafflingly—considered her many virtues.

He was into her. Big time.

How had she missed it?

Had the haze of her frustration obscured who he really was, how he really felt, from her? Or had he totally hidden his feelings while she'd dated another man?

She didn't know, just as she didn't quite know what to do with those feelings. Whether she should rebuff them as gently as possible or explore what they might mean for her. For them.

Because yes, she could almost smell the ozone from the electricity they were generating. But she'd also spent the last several months mired in anger and frustration because of him. She'd cried after her shifts and cursed his name and prayed he'd contract a heinous cold and miss a week of work.

Maybe the next several days would help her find the right way forward. She hoped so, because right now, she didn't know what the hell to do.

But she did know how to feel.

Cherished. Lustful. And above all else, awful.

Absolutely, completely awful.

Because all those months she'd been bitching about him to her friends and silently fuming to herself under a pasted-on smile at the desk, he'd been admiring her perfume and leather boots and marveling at her librarian abilities.

Maybe he'd deserved her rancor; maybe he hadn't.

Either way, it didn't feel good to have disliked a kind, decent man who said her smile blinded him and her anger could stop the tides. Who held her like treasure. And no matter what she decided to do about him—about them—she was never, ever going to complain about him again.

He didn't need to know about her issues with his work style.

And he definitely didn't need to know she'd once dreaded the very sight of him.

She needed to do what she always did: keep her mouth shut.

"Now kiss each other," Gladys ordered.

Or maybe not.

But to Callie's shock, Thomas gently disengaged himself from her and rose to his full height. The removal of his warm hands, his lean body, left her chilled in the stale air conditioning of the meeting room.

"No," he said.

His voice was firm. Not distracted. Not even especially good-natured.

Gladys raised her brows once again. "You're not willing to kiss her?"

Oh, Lord, he was going to give them away. Gladys would call Irene and say they weren't a couple after all, and then they'd be booted from the sh—

"That's not for the cameras." His blue gaze caught Callie's, and she was swimming in syrup. "That's for us."

The word—no, the *vow*—shivered through Callie in a ripple of heat.

The camerawoman heaved a sigh and turned away from them. "Then we're done here. Lord help me, romantics are the *worst*."

Which implied Gladys didn't think they were fakers. She

thought they were being *romantic*. Overly precious, yes, but definitely a couple.

Whew. Such a relief.

Although Callie wouldn't have minded a kiss from Thomas, cameras or no cameras. And maybe the disappointment slumping her shoulders told her everything she needed to know right now.

She might be a worrier, but she wasn't a fool.

She wasn't going to rebuff him.

She wasn't going to dwell on those months of frustration and annoyance.

She was going to spend a week in paradise with a kind, smart, handsome man who evidently adored her.

And she was going to discover what they could be. Together. Despite her worries.

"I suppose it's tour time, then." Thomas took her hand, and she curled her fingers around his, reveling in his strength. His warmth. "Are you ready?"

She lifted her chin to get a good view, beamed a smile at him, and watched his rapid blinking with satisfaction. "I'm ready."

THOMAS PUT HIS HAND OVER HIS MIC AND LEANED close.

"What do you think so far?" he asked quietly. Too quietly for the crew to pick up his words, especially over the ambient noise of the crowds and the surf.

The breeze from the water tugged strands free from Callie's ponytail and set them dancing around her face, and she was pretty sure her nose was turning pink under the bright sun and cloudless sky, despite a liberal coating of SPF 45. To the right, aquamarine waves descended in rhythmic rushes against ripples of golden sand, carefully manicured gardens to the left teemed with vibrant hibiscuses and lilies, and her hand was still securely clasped in Thomas's careful grip.

He and Callie, along with their HATV crew, had toured a good chunk of the private island already. The massive central hotel with its pink stucco and arches and the private cabanas tucked beneath palms. The water park. The water sports rental facility. The mirror-calm water of the noisy children's beach and the quiet, umbrella-strewn expanse of the adults-only beach. Various upscale restaurants, all with bird-themed names. The lavish theater with thickly cushioned seats and regular showtimes for the Parrot Cay Spectacular.

This episode of *Island Match* was going to be a hell of an advertisement for the destination, not that such a popular site needed any help.

Under the steady regard of the two cameras pointed at them, though, Callie hesitated to answer Thomas's question, even if no one but him could hear her answer.

He was going to think she was weird and ungrateful.

He was going to tell her she needed to relax.

After all, this was the cleanest place she'd ever seen. Including hospitals. And every single Parrot Cay employee greeted them with a wide smile, nodded, and wished them a *parrot-tastic day*. Whatever that meant. But they seemed sincere, if intense.

Very, very intense.

Like, freakily intense.

Okay, she had to say something. Before the two of them became ritual sacrifices to some beaked god.

Callie got up on her tiptoes to whisper in Thomas's ear. "I swear to God, that animatronic parrot is still watching us. The one just inside the theater door."

To his credit, he didn't quibble. Instead, he immediately

glanced back at the building's entrance. "Its beak *is* pointing in our direction."

"And have you noticed that three separate people in parrot costumes are following us?" When he twisted around again, she tugged on his sleeve and hissed, "Don't let them know we've spotted them."

Their tour guide, whose slicked-back bun had not budged an inch even after an hour-long tour, offered them a gleaming smile. "Do you have a question or concern? Because all of your friends here on Parrot Cay would be delighted to assist you in any way possible to guarantee the most parrot-tastic day of your life."

The woman wasn't even sweating. She didn't appear to have pores.

She'd introduced herself as Birdie. *Birdie*, for God's sake.

She was either an android or had sold her soul to parrot Beelzebub.

Thomas eyed Callie for a moment, and then swiveled to look at Birdie. "Callie's nose is burning. Why don't we wrap up the tour and take a break in our room before dinner?"

"Of course." Birdie's smile somehow widened, and sunlight glinted off her perfectly straight, perfectly white teeth. "We'll finish up in the pavilion, where Callie can find some shade, and I'll locate some aloe for her nose."

Callie released a long breath. "Thank you."

"Sunburns aren't very parrot-tastic." Their guide ushered them into the large, gazebo-like structure. "Thus, they are unacceptable."

Callie turned big eyes to Thomas, who squeezed her hand reassuringly.

Ten minutes later, she'd managed to present a creditable list of all the positive aspects of the island on camera, as had Thomas. When prompted by the crew for any negatives, she'd also noted, haltingly, that perhaps the atmosphere wasn't quite as *relaxed* as she'd hoped.

At that, Birdie's smile had frozen in place, her blank eyes pinned to Callie as three separate costumed parrots drew nearer, and Callie had almost fled in terror.

Thomas had echoed most of Callie's sentiments, while also noting his enjoyment of the various places on the grounds with hidden parrot paraphernalia, there to surprise and delight guests as they explored the island. After that, he'd hustled her back to the main hotel, a gentle hand at the small of her back, waving off Birdie's increasingly insistent offers of aloe.

The camera crew promised to meet them in an hour for dinner, and suddenly they were alone in the elevator and the long, white, pristine hall leading to their room.

The carpet was patterned with beady-eyed parrots, all eyeing her speculatively.

Then, finally, they were at the room. When Thomas couldn't find his key, Callie fumbled for hers, waited for the green light, and basically shoved him inside. Then she flipped the lock behind them and let out a slow breath.

Thomas headed straight for the bathroom. "I actually packed aloe. I would've said so, but I was concerned Birdie would deem it insufficiently parrot-tastic and confiscate the bottle."

Despite her lingering unease, Callie had to snicker at that.

For the first time in an hour, her shoulders dropped below her ears, and her breathing slowed. She sat on the edge of the bed with a sigh, watching Thomas.

After washing his hands, he wet a washcloth in the sink and unearthed a bottle of blue gel from his toiletry bag. Then he returned to the bed with the aloe and the cloth, unsealed the bottle, and crouched in front of her.

He held up the washcloth. "May I?"

Her throat dry, she nodded.

Lightly, he dabbed at her nose with the cool, damp cloth. "I didn't think the aloe would work as well through a layer of sand."

Speechless, she stared at him as he tended to her, dabbing until he was satisfied that he'd removed the grit from her skin. After squeezing a dollop of gel onto his finger, he spread it over her nose in gentle taps, and she sighed at the immediate relief.

He capped the bottle and remained crouched in front of her. "Better?"

God, he was a sweetheart of a man.

"Better. Thank you." She bit her lower lip. "I just don't know about this place, Thomas. I know it sounds horrible and ungrateful and selfish, because we're getting this trip for free, but—"

"You're not horrible." He rose to his feet and sat next to her on the bed, that hair-dusted thigh of his only inches away from hers. "You're under no obligation to like anything, Callie, ever. Not even if it's free. Not even if other people like it. Your feelings are your feelings."

Why did that statement, firm but softly spoken, make her eyes sting?

If she could tell anyone, she could tell him. He felt…

Well, he felt *safe*. In a way Andre never had, even at the beginning.

"It's just…" She studied the frayed hem of his olive-green shorts, unable to meet his gaze. "I have issues with anxiety sometimes. So it can be hard for me to tell if there's really a problem, or whether I'm just overreacting to something."

He touched her forearm with a fingertip. "I had no idea."

"I try to keep a handle on it." Raising her chin, she issued her plea face-to-face. "Please don't say anything to anyone at work."

"I wouldn't. I promise." His dark brows had drawn tight in concern. "I'm just sorry you have to struggle with something like that, because it sounds difficult and"—he paused —"disorienting, I guess. Maybe isolating too, if you don't think you can tell anyone."

Her next breath came without as much strain.

He got it. Maybe not completely, but the basic contours of the problem.

"Yes," she said quietly. "All those things."

His little nod of acknowledgment somehow eased her breathing even more. "So tell me what's worrying you, then." He fell back on the bed and braced himself on his elbows, giving her the superior position. Somehow, she didn't think that was a coincidence.

She turned her head to track his movement, and there he was, his body spread out almost flat next to hers, his chest a warm, solid expanse beneath that thin blue tee. A display of masculine beauty in recline, lean and muscled. A temptation for her curious fingers, which twitched to explore the terrain.

But she and Thomas weren't there yet. Might never be there. So she needed to keep talking, if only to distract herself.

"I feel like we're at risk of being sacrificed to some parrot overlord or becoming Stepford Wives." She frowned, considering the matter. "Stepford Parrots, I mean. Everything is just so…controlled. Rehearsed. It makes me uncomfortable. And I get the sense that Parrot Cay keeps a very, very close eye on its guests. I don't like feeling watched all the time."

He flopped all the way to his back and rested his head on his palms, his elbows splayed to the sides. "I can understand that."

She waited a minute, but that was all he said. He didn't tell her to get over it. He didn't tell her she was mistaken or stupid. He didn't even ask her to justify her statements.

The relief of it stunned her. So much so that she flopped down beside him, onto the pillows, his elbow next to her ear.

So much so that her racing thoughts cleared, and she could dig a little deeper.

"But I'm not even sure those are my main issues, really." She let out a long breath. "I guess I don't like being watched by the camera crew all the time, either. Especially since we're lying, and I'm worried about getting caught. I'm worried about putting you in an uncomfortable position, and I'm worried about what we'll be expected to do to justify receiving this trip. And it's hard for me to be in an unfamiliar environment, especially when I'm already tense."

That was the central irony, wasn't it? In her desperation to seize a sandy, sun-soaked week of recovery from the work and stress of the last few years, she'd invented a relationship with Thomas. But—perhaps fittingly—both the lie and the television show enabling the trip had transformed it into an additional, potent source of worry for her. Maybe for him, too.

Her throat had gone tight. "All this is just…"

He waited patiently, without trying to fill in the words for her.

"It's a lot," she finally said. "It's a lot to handle, especially for someone like me."

The rooms in the hotel must be well-insulated, because she couldn't hear anything for a few seconds but the whoosh of the air-conditioning and her heartbeat.

In the fraught silence, her thoughts spiraled.

Maybe he hated being put in this position. Maybe all her complaints, all her worries were too much for him. Maybe this entire trip had been an enormous mistake from the beginning.

Then he levered up on one elbow and looked down into her eyes, his lean face solemn. "Two things. First, you never have to worry about putting me in an uncomfortable position. I don't suffer silently, and I'd be more than willing to talk to the HATV crew if either one of us had concerns about what was happening. In general, very few things make me uncomfortable, so please stop devoting headspace to that issue."

She raised her brows at him.

He sighed. "Sorry. I imagine that's easier said than done."

"Yup."

His dark curls had rumpled in the island breeze, and flecks of sand shone on his cheekbones as the rosy light of the setting sun filtered through the gleaming windows and washed over his face. The creases across his forehead indicated his concentration.

On her. He was focused on her with such intensity, she wanted to bask in it.

"Which brings me to my second point." He leaned over a bit, until just a thread of his grassy scent sent her pulse wobbling. "What do you need from me?"

He was in the edges of her space now, his face in her vision and his body a protective bulwark beside hers, and she couldn't answer his question.

Pretending to be a couple today had proven easier than she'd anticipated. So easy she couldn't tell the difference between what was genuinely happening between them and what was happening for the cameras, yet another reason for her confusion and concern.

But they were alone now, with no cameras and no boom mic and no producer. No tight-smiled tour guides or animatronic parrots with glassy eyes.

And he was still just as gentle. Just as attentive. Just as…

She could say it, if only to herself.

Just as *loving*.

So what did she need from him?

Everything. She needed everything.

But right now, everything would also scare the hell out of her, and she knew it.

His gaze skirted the length of her on the bed, just once, and his throat bobbed as he swallowed hard. Then he clarified himself, his voice a husky rasp, a flush cresting his cheekbones. "When you're worried, do you need me to reassure you? Do you need me to try to fix whatever problems you might have? Or do you just need me to listen?"

Oh. That question she could answer. And she loved that he was asking it. That he didn't have any preconceived ideas about how to deal with her worries, and he was letting her guide him in such an important matter.

There he was, asking for direction in the hopes of pleasing her. His eyes intent on her and her alone.

She shouldn't think it. She really shouldn't. But she couldn't help it.

If they made love, would he be as attentive? As eager to please?

It was her turn to swallow past a dry throat. "Just listen, please. Thank you for asking."

His blue eyes had turned nearly incandescent with heat as they studied her expression. Then, in one jerky motion, he sat up and swung his legs over the side of the bed, facing away from her.

"Do you feel any better?" Thomas's voice was rough. "Or do you want me to contact the crew and tell them we need more time before dinner?"

To her surprise, she actually did feel better. Even though they hadn't actually solved any of her problems, the simple act of discussing them had settled her. Eased her more comfortably into her own skin.

Or maybe she was simply distracted from her worries by sheer animal lust.

"Much better." She laid a hand flat on his back, and his breath hitched. "Because of you."

"I'm glad." His breathing had become audible in the room, his triceps bunching as he gripped the edge of the bed.

If she didn't want to push this further, she needed to let him go.

So she did, the loss of contact an ache.

They sat in silence for a minute.

"Did you know that the founder of Parrot Cay, Weebly Dixon, had a pet parrot he trained to eat from his mouth?" When he spoke again, Thomas sounded more like himself, amused and calm. "He left all his money and property to her, much to his widow's dismay. And the parrot's name was—"

"Don't tell me." Callie groaned. "Birdie. Of course."

"There were unsavory rumors. Rival developers called Birdie his Parrot Paramour."

Callie thought for a moment. "Shouldn't she have been his Bird of Paradise?"

He looked over his shoulder and grinned at her. "Nice."

He'd been offering similar tidbits for her amusement all day, products of the research he'd done for their trip. And now that she wasn't hustling to serve a growing line of patrons as he slowpoked his way through the archives, she could remember why she'd once sought him out at every opportunity, eager to hear whatever fascinating or funny story he had to offer.

Today, she'd noticed something new about him. Whenever she laughed, he did too. And every time, he ducked his head in the most adorable way. As if he were hiding his amusement from the world and keeping it private, only shared between the two of them. But then he'd sneak a glance up at her, as if glorying in her hilarity. As if he'd worked for it and was proud of it.

Maybe he had. Maybe he was.

This particular story, though, had served an additional purpose. Distraction.

And distraction was welcome, because soon they'd need to wash up and leave for dinner. They'd chat and eat and film some bits for the show.

Then they'd come back to the room. To the king-sized bed. Alone.

And she had no idea what would happen then.

FOUR

THOMAS MADE HIS ESCAPE IN THE PRE-DAWN darkness.

Last night—his first spent beside Callie—he'd rushed to shower before her, donned a tee and pajama bottoms, and burrowed under the covers in deep, feigned sleep before she'd emerged from her own bedtime routines in the bathroom.

He'd kept his breathing steady and his body motionless, even when he'd heard her quiet whisper of his name. Even when he'd felt himself sinking into the hazy pleasure of sharing a bed with Callie Adesso, the woman he desired with shocking urgency.

Unprecedented, all-encompassing urgency.

He'd only had a handful of women in his life and his arms, and he'd cared about them. But despite his best intentions and efforts, they'd always drifted away from him. Because, they said, he'd drifted away first. Into his own thoughts and ideas and interests. Into a headspace where he didn't pay attention to them, to anything, the way he should.

Or maybe drifted away wasn't the right description, since

they'd told him—and he knew they were right—he'd never really been present. Not as they'd deserved and needed.

He'd grieved. He'd been ashamed. He'd been lonely at times and resigned to more loneliness to come.

He hadn't known how to fix whatever was broken inside him.

But when he'd met Callie, the click had almost been audible.

There was no subject that would banish her completely from his thoughts. No mental games that could engross him so wholly that he would forget her existence for hours at a time. No distraction from her presence.

Especially now that they were sharing a bed.

He couldn't focus on anything but the soft whoosh of her breathing. The heat that radiated from her lush body and gathered beneath the covers. The citrusy smell of the hotel-provided body wash, which had turned warmer and more alluring as it mingled with her own scent. And, when he'd woken in the middle of the night, the pale gleam and abundant curves of her velvety flesh by moonlight.

Her sleeveless, floaty nightgown might have been born from his fantasies. And in her restless sleep, she kept kicking free from the covers and sprawling across the bed in disarray, that nightgown bunched around her round thighs and climbing.

Ever-changing and ever-fascinating in sleep, as in wakefulness. He should've known.

Still, he'd turned his back to the sight and gripped the edge of the bed to ensure he didn't move closer. And he'd made sure to rise before her, get dressed in the dark, and leave the room before she could awaken.

At this time of the morning, the hotels halls were silent, and the camera crew was nowhere to be found. The lounge chairs by the shore were empty, the golden sands empty of anyone but a few employees raking bits of errant seaweed into piles. No doubt seaweed was not considered parrot-tastic enough to tolerate.

Also, he was pretty sure he could spot one of the costumed parrots in the distance, partially hidden behind some palms, its beak pointed his way.

No matter. He suspected they saved any ritual sacrifices for the nightly Parrot Cay Spectacular, which didn't occur for many hours yet. He should be safe.

He reclined the chair, stretched his legs out on the cushioned seat, let the salty ocean air fill his lungs, and watched the steady rush of the gentle waves until the urgency of his need receded like the tide. In its place, reason slowly returned.

Yes, he wanted Callie with the single-minded desperation of a sailor in thrall to a siren's song. And yes, maybe she was beginning to want him too.

He hoped so, given the way she'd grazed his arm, his knee, even his chest, with light fingertips during dinner. The way she'd begun focusing that hot brown gaze on his mouth and biting her own lip. Even the way she'd held his hand and nestled close to his side as they made their way back to the hotel under the watchful eyes of the camera crew.

But that wasn't enough. Not given the shadow of uncertainty he still spied on her face every time they moved a step closer to one another. Not given how easy it would be for them both to confuse the forced intimacy of their deception with genuine desire on her part.

He wasn't making love with Callie—wasn't even kissing her—unless that shadow was gone and he knew she wanted *him*, not merely the man on this journey with her. If they were both obviously conscious and in bed together and she made an approach, though, he wasn't sure he could make himself say no.

Which was why he'd fled, before she blinked those brilliant eyes open and undid him once again. Just the thought of her turning to him, the sheets rustling in the quiet of a lazy morning, and shifting nearer with a soft smile of welcome—

Like the tide, his need returned. That vicious ache only Callie had ever inspired.

So he supposed he was going to watch the waves and read about a worldwide influenza pandemic for an hour or two, until he was certain she'd be awake and dressed. Until it was time to pack their bags, check out, and head to their next destination, Thongs.

Christ, another night in bed together was going to prove a stern test of his mettle.

But for the chance of a real future with Callie, he could withstand just about anything. Even the brutal undertow of his own desire.

"Wow," Callie said. "Does that chair…"

Thomas gave a short nod. "Yes. The seat vibrates. At different frequencies and intensities. The remote is tucked into a pocket on the side of the cushion, according to the guest handbook."

He'd tried reading that handbook to distract himself while Callie explored the suite. It wasn't helping.

"Huh." Running a hand over its plush velvet cover, she studied the armless chair and tilted her head in what appeared to be—God help him—intrigued speculation. "I guess I hadn't realized an adults-only island would be so flagrantly…uh, *adults-only*."

Their room, he'd found, was full of such unique features. *Unique* in the sense of *torturous*.

Callie trailed to the bed.

"That's a weird design on the headboard. Not very comfortable for sitting. Why would anyone put leather loops all over—" She trailed into silence. "Never mind."

Clearly, he'd underestimated the problematic nature of the second island on their itinerary. But in his defense, the destination's logo was a pair of flip-flops entangled with one another. I.e., thongs.

He hadn't realized that Thongs was about flip-flops in the same way Hooters was about nocturnal birds of prey. And he definitely hadn't anticipated the wholehearted commitment of Thongs's staff and owners to hedonism. Also to Georgia O'Keeffe paintings and leather.

But his mistake had become evident very, very rapidly. Immediately upon their arrival at the island's dock, in fact.

A limousine had been waiting for them. One with an opaque glass partition the driver—after showing them flutes of chilled champagne and a crystal bowl of condoms—had pointedly raised after noting its soundproof design.

At the last moment, she'd rolled it back down for a final comment. "Wet wipes are in the right lower cabinet."

Then up the glass had gone again, while Callie choked and began coughing. Thomas had closed his eyes in distinct pain while bracing her with a hand spread wide on her warm, silk-covered back. Other than those coughs, the short ride to the hotel had been very silent. But that silence had been thick. Stifling. And he hadn't been able to force himself to move his hand, not for the whole ride. She hadn't shifted away from him, either.

Instead, she'd pressed back against the seat, as if trapping his hand. Increasing the intensity of the contact.

So he should have comprehended the disastrous nature of the situation then. Or if not then, when the crew had arrived too, and he and Callie strode into the hotel lobby on camera, the boom mic overhead, and saw the statuary.

Her cheeks had gone ruddy, but for the first time on their trip, she'd seemed to forget about the crew. No, she'd been too busy studying the various configurations of marble humans in congress with other marble humans—interspersed with a few marble satyrs and other similar creatures —to pay attention to Gladys or anyone else.

To be fair, filming had largely come to a halt, because HATV was meant to be a family-friendly network. But Callie hadn't even appeared to notice the moment when the cameras lowered to the floor and the boom mic guy wandered off toward the lobby's tray of chocolate-covered strawberries.

"I'd dislocate a hip," he'd heard her mumble at one erotic display.

He hadn't said a word. Even attempts to remember colonial tax policy couldn't help him under this sort of strain. So in lieu of saying something he shouldn't, he simply followed her without a word, like a lust-struck shadow.

At another tableau composed of gleaming stone flesh, she'd spent some time eyeing the scene's participants. Her mouth opened, then closed. Then opened again.

"Where would he even put his…" A pause. "Oh. I forget about that option."

Dear Lord.

"Why don't we check in?" he'd suggested at that point, hoarse desperation in every syllable he managed to utter. "We have dinner reservations soon."

"He's right." Gladys had sounded a bit stressed too. "We need time to set up in the restaurant before then. Hopefully someplace without so many marble dongs on display."

Thank goodness for Gladys, voice of sanity.

"And we reserved you a VIP booth at Club Carnal for your after-dinner activity," she'd continued, "so wear the sexiest clothes you brought. Within network-standards reason."

Gladys, you foul betrayer.

They'd checked in. The crew had followed them down hallways papered with textured cherry-red brocade and filmed a few quick shots of the suite, some of which might even be suitable for children. And then the HATV people had left, abandoning Thomas to his torment like the traitors they were.

Callie had stopped fondling the headboard, thank goodness, but she was eyeing him closely, her thick brows drawn.

"You've been very quiet." She took a step toward him. "Are you okay?"

"Just a bit tired," he said.

The truth. He hadn't had much sleep the night before, and he didn't anticipate much more rest that night. Especially given what he'd just read about the contents of the nightstands.

Her scrutiny didn't waver, and he fought a shudder at how that steady, concentrated perusal burned through his clothing like a shower of embers. How her mere proximity made him weak, made him hard, in the dim hush of a room designed for pleasure.

She waved a hand, encompassing their surroundings in a single graceful sweep. "Does all this make you uncomfrotable?"

Definitely. But perhaps not for the reasons she might imagine, and not for reasons he was willing to discuss with her at that moment.

He countered the question with its echo. "Does it make *you* uncomfortable?"

When she blinked and glanced away, he could finally draw oxygen to his lungs again.

"Not really." Her voice sounded steady. Definite. "With anyone else, I would be super-anxious right now. Worried about what HATV might want us to do on this island.

Worried about what my…" She cleared her throat. "Worried about what my partner would want from me, and how much of it would end up on camera."

The idea of her pressured into situations that made her anxious, ones she didn't choose or want, made his gut clench.

Callie's voice interrupted his thoughts. "But I know you would speak up if the crew requested something that made me uncomfortable, because you did that already, during our first photo shoot." Her brows compressed again, and her lips pinched a tad. "And you were a total gentleman last night. This morning, too. It felt like we were hardly in the same room together, much less in the same bed."

Her gaze landed on the huge slab of mattress dominating their suite. She reached out to caress the slick wine-colored silk of their comforter, and all the blessed oxygen departed his lungs in a whoosh.

"So no, I'm not uncomfortable." Another step toward him. Another. Until she was within arm's reach, her chin tipped up to him and her glossy lips parted. "But I still don't know whether *you're* uncomfortable. Some people might find all this"—she gestured to their surroundings again —"shocking or off-putting, and if you're one of them, I want you to know that's totally okay. If you'd like, we can talk to Gladys about finding a different place to stay tonight."

He exhaled through his nose.

Really, he shouldn't be surprised. Not by her thoughtfulness, nor by her concern. From the beginning, their coworkers had assumed his absentmindedness, his academic bent, the way he didn't seem to notice the world around him while he sorted through his thoughts, his research, his ideas, meant he must be an innocent or a prude. Possibly someone entirely uninterested in sex.

He hadn't dated anyone since starting at CMRL, which

had only confirmed that mistaken belief. A belief that, apparently, Callie might share.

There was nothing wrong with being innocent or asexual.

But he wasn't either, and he wanted her to know that.

"Callie..." When he moved a step closer, her breath feathered across his neck in a ticklish rush. Carefully, he lifted a hand and traced the silken heat of her cheek with his knuckles, and her eyes flew to his, dark and wide. "I'm no monk."

Her teeth sank into her lower lip. "You're not?"

"No." He stroked the line of her jaw, the tempting length of her vulnerable neck. Her flesh rippled into goosebumps beneath the light drag of his knuckles. "Definitely not."

He really wasn't.

And if they didn't leave the room soon, he was going to beg her to let him prove it.

He allowed himself one last gift. A slow sweep of his thumb across that distracting, plump lower lip, which lowered in a shuddering breath.

Then he forced himself to step away, even though the carpet beneath his feet had dissolved into quicksand. "We should get ready for dinner."

She stood there for a moment, her expression dazed and her eyes cloudy, as he hustled to his suitcase. But when he whacked his knee against the leg of the desk—waist-height and very sturdy, he'd unwillingly noted—she startled and gave him a sympathetic wince.

"That looked like it hurt." She dropped onto the mattress in a sudden descent, as if her own knees had given way. "Are you all right?"

He carefully kept his back to her as he zipped open his bag. "I'm fine."

In fact, the pain was distracting him from discomfort in other areas of his anatomy, which was a welcome development.

After that, they each took a turn changing in the absurdly lavish bathroom, which boasted heated floors. Marble sinks. An enormous, sybaritic shower. A sunken bathtub big enough for a crowd.

His gaze caught on one of the shower's adjustable body jets, which would hit at about his upper thighs. But for Callie, if she was facing the jet and he was behind her, spreading her open for the spray—

He gripped the marble countertop with both hands, bracing himself there as he dropped his chin to his chest and got himself under control.

It was going to be a long, steamy night.

And not just because he and Callie had traveled to a tropical paradise.

FIVE

CALLIE DEFINITELY PREFERRED THOMAS TO THE male strippers.

She'd seen a number of the performers up close—*really* close, since the resort had given them prime seats in Club Carnal—so she was in an enviable position to judge.

Yes, their muscles bulged. Yes, their chests were as smooth as that silky passion fruit crème anglaise she'd had with dessert. Yes, they could thrust their hips with startling vigor, at an impressive frequency, and without any signs of tiring, not even after pretending to be dance-loving, clothing-averse firefighters for several impressive, athletic minutes.

And yes, maybe that Clark Kent-esque one with the glasses and the tearaway shirt and bowtie—not to mention the gleaming, tree-trunk thighs—would have turned her crank a week ago.

But Clark Kent didn't freeze in place and stop speaking mid-word when he first saw her dressed for the evening. He didn't tell her she looked like an Amazon queen in her goddess dress and gladiator sandals, or marvel at how she'd tamed her hair into a twist. He didn't listen to every word she said at dinner as if she were an oracle predicting the fate of humanity. He didn't drop his fork on the floor when she smiled at him.

Clark Kent didn't check to make sure she was comfortable seeing the strip show before it began. He didn't sit beside her during that strip show without any evidence of discomfort or attempts to reaffirm his heterosexuality.

Clark Kent was hot, no doubt about it, but his glasses didn't make him look like an ancient history professor who'd cause a stampede of hungry women to return to college, or perhaps a lit professor whose handsome, gentle face would inspire a thousand sonnets, all composed during class. And his suit didn't skim the slim, strong lines of his frame in a way that made her want to explore such gorgeous, unfamiliar terrain in detail, in privacy, and in totality. While naked.

So she didn't want Clark Kent. She wanted Thomas. More than she'd ever imagined she could.

When the club DJ played her first slow song after the end of the strip show, Thomas stood. He reached out a hand and invited Callie to dance with him. And when she accepted, he folded her into his arms and cradled her like a priceless artifact made of glass.

They were swaying to Sade, one of the artist's older tracks, the gentle, seductive warmth of her voice a partner in the dance. Callie looped her arms around Thomas's neck, the better to draw him close. Preferably, as close as her next breath. And his hands…

Oh, goodness. One of them was braced, firm and warm, on her back. Supporting her. Guiding her away from other oblivious couples and the tables edging the dance floor.

But the other hand…it was playing at the nape of her neck. Stroking. Kneading softly. Tracing the fine wisps of hair that had escaped her updo.

She was on the verge of combustion, despite a hazy awareness of the cameras filming their every move.

As the song continued, he nearly tripped over a speaker wire, and his sway slowed to a near stop. But he nudged her away from that same wire, and those gentle, talented hands of his didn't falter for a moment.

She got it. Finally, she got it.

When Thomas concentrated on something, on someone, the rest of his world disappeared. At the library, that meant she worked alone, even as she worked beside him. On the ferry to Parrot Cay, that meant he was paying so much attention to her, he nearly fell overboard. Here, in her arms, it meant he was so focused on holding her that he forgot to watch his feet, or even move them.

He wanted her. This strong, sweet, protective man who'd made her laugh dozens of times during dinner and couldn't seem to do anything in a hurry.

She sincerely hoped that applied to foreplay too.

When the music faded, he spoke into her ear. "It's getting late. Do you want to go back to our room?"

Oh, yes. She really did.

He held her hand as they said good night to the crew. All the way to the elevator, all the way down the hall to their door. But when they got inside their room, he gave her fingers a squeeze and let them go.

He beamed that sweet, affectionate smile her way. "May I take a shower first?"

To her shock, he gathered what he needed and shut the bathroom doors behind him. The sound of running water began moments later.

He'd left her with no kiss. No loaded glances. No seductive invitation to join him in the shower.

Had she misunderstood everything? Mistaken on-camera

flirtation and the affectionate gestures of a friend for something different?

She was still standing there frozen, just inside the room, when he emerged from the bathroom minutes later, dressed in a thin white tee and drawstring pajama bottoms.

"Your turn." He smiled at her again. "We have a tour scheduled early in the morning, so we should get some sleep. You must be exhausted." Then he flipped back the covers on his side of the bed and climbed inside, turning so his back was to her and his voice was muffled when he spoke again. "Thank you for a truly wonderful day, Callie. One of the best I've ever had."

She'd hoped for a truly wonderful night too. One of the best she'd ever had.

But it appeared that wasn't going to happen, so she choked out a pro forma but honest reply. "Same here."

In a sudden, embarrassed hurry, she kicked off her shoes, grabbed a nightgown from her suitcase, walked to the bathroom, and closed the doors behind her. The dress she hung on a hook to prevent wrinkles. The bra and panties she kicked to the corner.

A quick shower washed away the glowy goddess makeup she'd applied earlier that evening and the grime inevitable after a day of travel. The body jets pummeled her skin until she felt raw, and even the soft towels provided by the hotel abraded her oversensitive flesh.

Her hair unraveled after the removal of a few strategic bobby pins, falling around her shoulders. The simple shift nightgown floated over her head, and there she was in the mirror.

Not an Amazon queen.

Just Callie. Confused and worried, with dark circles under her eyes and a furrow pinched between her brows.

She braced herself before opening the bathroom door. But

just like the previous night, only her bedside lamp was illuminated, Thomas had turned his back to her, and he wasn't moving or speaking.

Asleep or feigning it.

It didn't really matter which. Even if he was faking, she clearly didn't have the ovaries to press him on it. So instead of whispering his name, as she'd done the previous night, she simply climbed into the empty side of the bed, turned out her light, and resigned herself to another restless night in which Thomas remained simultaneously too close and too far.

GLADYS WAS LISTING THE AFTERNOON'S ITINERARY, her voice rising above the sound of the boat's engine and the splash of waves against its two hulls. "Upon our arrival on Renaissance Island, we'll immediately take a private tour of the grounds and facilities. Then, after we check in, you two will go parasailing, followed by dinner at Seaside Steaks restaurant. After dinner, you have tickets to—"

Callie nodded automatically, her mind elsewhere.

Just minutes ago, they'd completed a very risqué tour of Thongs—which had included an illuminating stop at the very special adult toy store on the island—and boarded a catamaran ferry to the third and final island they'd visit.

Renaissance Island. The entire reason she'd applied to *Island Match*.

Under a cloudless sky, the boat was skimming over the water, full of laughing tourists and amiable crew members. The sun's reflection off the whitecaps seared into her retinas, and the breeze tempered the heat of a summer day off the coast of Florida.

Somewhere over the horizon, their destination waited.

She should be excited. Carefree. Marking every word Gladys said with strict attention.

But Callie had already reviewed the schedule that morning. She didn't really need to listen. Which was convenient, since she wasn't listening. Couldn't listen. Not with Thomas so near and her mind so cluttered.

He stood behind her, his butt propped against the wooden rail, his arms looped around her waist and her body tucked into the curve of his. It seemed to be a protective position, as if he were attempting to ensure she didn't get jostled and tumble overboard.

Which, to be honest, she found sort of hilarious. If anyone was going to fall off the boat and into the ridiculously blue water, he was the most likely candidate. No question about it.

Still, she appreciated the gesture. And since that ridiculously blue water matched his eyes exactly, she was also experiencing a pleasant sense of vindication. She snapped a quick picture of the water with her cell phone to send Cowan and Irene later that day.

"Look at me for a moment," she whispered to Thomas.

He did, and she snapped a photo of his eyes.

Uh-huh. Perfect match.

Gladys paused. "Did you hear that last bit, Callie?"

Nope. "Yup."

That fleeting moment of victory past, her worries crept back into her thoughts. By the time she surfaced and took conscious stock of her surroundings once more, Gladys had finished talking and gone elsewhere. So had the hair and makeup woman. Other than the camera operators and boom mic guy, Callie and Thomas were alone at the rail.

He was turning her in his arms and nudging her chin upwards with a single, careful fingertip. He studied her face, his high forehead creased with worry.

"Are you okay?" The words were a quiet murmur, pitched too low for the mic. "You seem...not entirely present."

Well, of all people, he would know how that felt.

She too kept her voice quiet. "Was it obvious I wasn't listening?"

"Not really. Other than when you took your pictures, I don't think Gladys noticed." Those startling blue eyes searched hers. "You made all the right responses, but you didn't sound like yourself. What's going on?"

She bit her lip. What she had to say didn't belong on camera, but she needed to talk.

"I'm worried," she finally whispered.

He inclined his head in acknowledgment, and then immediately addressed the nearby crew. "Please give us a few minutes."

To their credit, they didn't grumble as they departed. Probably because the ferry captain had just announced the availability of unlimited rum punch and fresh fruit on toothpicks under the covered part of the deck.

Then Thomas pulled her tight against his body and looked down at her with his Listening Face. Calm. Patient. Accepting. Interested.

His Listening Face made her want to see his Kissing Face. But there was no time for that, even if he'd welcome her mouth on his. She had to take advantage of this opportunity to talk, because she might not get another for hours to come.

She knew that for a fact, since this was their first truly private moment all day.

For the second morning in a row, Thomas had woken before her and left the room without waking her. Which, frankly, was a miracle, given how often that man fumbled and tripped over things. And for the second morning in a row, he hadn't returned until she was already dressed and ready for the day, the cameras poised and hovering nearby.

On Parrot Cay, his absence when she'd woken had felt like a relief. A way to avoid potential awkwardness. And she'd appreciated how he hadn't pushed her into intimacy, how he'd remained sensitive to any privacy concerns she might have.

This morning, though…

His absence had frustrated her. Disappointed her.

She'd wanted to discover how Thomas looked first thing in the morning, still rumpled and warm and sleepy. She'd wanted to feel the frisson of possibility when they woke in the same bed, only inches apart. She'd wanted to see all the goodness his Kissing Face had to offer.

To be honest, she'd wanted more than Kissing Face. Considerably more. Maybe even Lovemaking Face.

But most of all, she'd simply wanted to talk to him. Because she was concerned and stressed about the day ahead, and talking it out with someone she trusted might help.

His ability to listen was off-the-charts phenomenal. Now that she'd experienced how it felt to have his total concentration directed her way, she wanted more. Much more.

No wonder all the patrons went to him. In their buckled shoes, she'd do the same.

"Callie?" The stroke of his thumb along her cheek grounded her. Brought her out of her head and back into reality. "Talk to me."

She spoke in a blurted rush, the words jumbled and breathless. "I know I signed waivers and agreed to everything, and I don't want to mess things up for the crew or make their jobs harder, but I wish I didn't have to follow the itinerary for the day."

He nodded and didn't say anything.

"The thought of parasailing makes my stomach churn. Whoever tries to buckle me into my harness better be wearing washable fabrics, because I'll probably throw up all over them." She ticked her other concerns off her fingers. "I don't like steak. Tess tells me the show we're going to see is serviceable, but not spectacular. And I don't think I can absorb another tour without at least one good night's sleep beforehand."

He tilted his head. "Who's Tess?"

"A friend who recently visited Renaissance Island." And snagged a much-younger, former-tennis-pro boyfriend during that visit, but that was a subject for a different conversation. "She and April talked to me about everything they saw, everything they did. They're the reason I wanted to go on *Island Match* in the first place. Their descriptions made the island sound..."

She splayed her hand on his chest and thought for a moment. "They made it sound magical. Peaceful. Quiet. Like a place where I could clear my head and get my feet beneath me again."

His brows drew together at the last part, but he didn't pursue the remark. "So you planned to pick this third island from the beginning?"

"From the first moment." She snuck a glance at Gladys, who appeared to be enjoying the supply of free drinks. "But nothing I actually want to do, nothing that would bring me joy or peace, is on our itinerary. And yes, if you're willing to go along with my plan, I know we'll have three more days here, but I may not survive until then. Parasailing equipment isn't made for people built like me, and I'm beyond terrified of heights."

She curled her fingers in his tee and summed up the situation. "I want to sit in clear, warm water and let the waves rock me back and forth until my brain quiets. I want to take a nap in the shade of a palm. I want to get a massage. I want to order room service. I want to eat more red snapper, because that fish was freaking delicious. I want to meet Tess's new boyfriend, so I can determine whether he's good enough for her. I want to go on a cruise around the island."

He was quiet. Concentrating solely on her, his eyes tempting and deep enough for her to drown in them.

"I don't even care if cameras are around for part of it. I just don't want crowds or tour guides or set schedules." She tugged at his fabric. "And I want to spend time with you. Private time."

She'd omitted her other, Thomas-specific worries. Her anxiety about whether she'd somehow misinterpreted his cues, about whether a romantic relationship with him would founder when they returned to work and he left her stranded on the desk, etc., etc.

Maybe someday she'd be brave enough to talk about those issues with him. But not now.

"That's it," she said. "That's why I'm anxious today."

His hand covered hers on his shirt, surrounding it with protective warmth. "Callie, is this a situation where discussing your worries is enough? Or should one of us do something?"

"Like talk to Gladys?" She grimaced and looked down at her sandals. "I don't know."

Ducking his head, he regained eye contact. "Why does that thought scare you?"

She had to laugh, the sound bitter even to her own ears. "Because I'm anxious, Thomas. Almost everything scares me, but especially confrontation. I hate making people angry or disappointed. Even the thought of it gives me hives."

"You think Gladys and the crew might be upset if you told them what you wanted?"

"Yes." She nodded. "And that's the problem."

Every time she considered asking Gladys to change the schedule, her heart kicked into a gallop, her breath grew short, and her chest started itching.

He thought for a moment. "How about we talk to her together? We can ask her whether the crew can accommodate what you want, at least for some of the day, without causing too much disruption. How does that sound?"

Her gaze snapped to his. "You don't have to do that. This isn't your problem."

But what a kind, wonderful offer. What a kind, wonderful man.

"Callie..." His hand tightened over hers. "I'm not like you. What other people think, what they might expect or want from me, doesn't concern me. But you do. I'm happy to talk to Gladys or the crew or the president of HATV or whomever. Anyone who can help you get what you need."

She had to admit he had a point. His mind clearly didn't work the same way as hers, as she'd lamented countless times over the previous six months. But she'd never imagined taking advantage of that often-frustrating difference.

"Besides, I want to spend time with you too." His lips curved in the sweetest expression of affection she'd ever witnessed. "Just the two of us. Do you want to find out whether we can make that happen?"

All she had to do was nod, and they were walking toward Gladys.

Ten minutes later, Callie had a new crop of hives on her chest. She also had a new itinerary for the next twenty-four hours, one that did *not* include death-defying heights over the cerulean waters.

Speaking up hadn't killed her. Almost, but not quite. Not with Thomas's quiet support.

With him by her side, everything seemed easier. Everything.

Even falling just a tiny bit in love.

SIX

THE NEXT MORNING, THOMAS SLEPT LONGER THAN Callie.

This was an unfortunate development.

He was coming to consciousness beside the hottest woman who'd ever existed. They were alone, in bed together, and nestled in what appeared to be a suite for honeymooners.

Worst of all, a sneaky squint through his eyelids established that she was awake and reading in bed, propped up against the quilted headboard. And from the look she was giving him right now, it appeared she'd caught his attempt at discreet observation.

He was screwed, and not in the way he'd have preferred.

"I know you're not asleep anymore," she said, closing the cover of her e-reader.

She'd opened one of the curtains partway while he'd been dozing, so even a squint revealed all the wonderful details. Her sweet face was still rosy with sleep, her dark hair rumpled and gleaming with fiery highlights in the morning sun. And that pale-pink nightgown flowed around her body in a way that hinted at the braless bounty beneath.

She was a ripe goddess who'd deigned to dally with mortals.

So he couldn't help but smile at her, even as he kept his eyelids mostly shut. "I might be. Perhaps I'm an inveterate sleep-squinter and sleep-talker. You can't be certain after only two nights."

She raised those thick, dark brows. "*Are* you a sleep-squinter? Or a sleep-talker?"

"No." His back cracked a bit as he stretched. "But I appreciate your asking."

A giggle escaped her in a little puff of breath, and he laughed with her as he sat up. And against his better judgment, he didn't spring out of bed and race to the bathroom, locking himself safely away from temptation. Instead, he too settled against the headboard, shifting until they were sitting thigh-to-thigh.

He stifled a yawn. "Have you been up long?"

When she twisted to face him, the neckline of her night-gown gaped a bit, exposing the top curve of her left breast. His yawn nearly turned into a groan of need.

"About an hour. I just couldn't sleep any longer." She shook her head. "I can't believe I collapsed into bed so early."

He could, given her restlessness the previous two nights. During their dinner at that seafood restaurant, her eyelids had been drooping, and at one point she'd nearly dropped face-first into her citrus-curd pavlova.

As soon as they'd arrived back at their room, she'd stumbled to the bathroom, washed up, and essentially fallen onto the mattress. By the time he'd emerged from his own bedtime routine, she'd been out for the night.

He considered that a blessing. She'd needed rest, and he'd needed to avoid spending time in bed with Callie while they were both conscious.

But he still wanted to find out whether she regularly had

trouble sleeping. Whether, given the opportunity and the right circumstances, he could relieve that restlessness in time-honored fashion.

And during the course of yet another long, sleepless night of his own, he'd had the chance to formulate other questions too. Important ones.

Do you ever feel anxious at work?

If so, she hadn't shown it. Then again, he'd watched her seem comfortable and confident during that lengthy tour of Parrot Cay and on the ferry to Renaissance Island, only to discover she'd been worrying the entire time about a panoply of issues. He now knew she was able to hide her emotional distress well. So well, he didn't know whether to applaud or grieve that she'd clearly had so much practice.

What went wrong a couple months after you started work at the CMRL? Were you stressed because of problems with Andre, or did something else happen?

Only upon Callie's arrival had he truly felt attached to anyone working there. But even that tie had become thin and frayed, for whatever reason.

A reason he still didn't understand. A reason he *needed* to understand.

But those questions would have to wait, because he and Callie had more urgent matters to address. Preferably before the luscious pressure of her body against his scuttled his resolve for good.

He cleared his throat. "As long as we have a few minutes alone, we should probably talk."

"Oh, Lord." Her groan vibrated through him. "Those words strike fear into the heart of any right-thinking person."

If she didn't want to talk, he wasn't going to force her. No matter how much he ached to declare himself.

He swung his legs over the side of the bed. "Never mind. We can talk later, if you'd prefer that."

"It's fine." With a sigh, she tugged his arm until he climbed back under the covers. "Let's get this over with. Quickly, if at all possible."

All right. The direct approach it was.

He took a fortifying breath and laid his heart bare. "I like you, Callie. Very much. Everything I said to Gladys during that interview, I meant. You're wondrous. Lovely and smart and kind and capable." He chanced a peek at her, just in time to see a rosy flush bloom on her cheeks. "I want you more than I've ever wanted anyone or anything. Which sounds generic and facile, but I mean it. I want you more than I wanted a completed dissertation and successful dissertation defense. More than I wanted a tenure-track position at a research university. More than I want my job at CMRL. So when I say I want you very much, I mean I could happily see nothing but your face, smell nothing but your perfume, touch nothing but your skin, and hear nothing but your voice for the rest of my life."

She'd been staring at him, her eyes wide. But at the last bit, she gave a tentative snort. "Just my face?"

"Maybe more than your face." He grinned at her. "Considerably more."

She scooted a bit closer, until the side of her breast pressed against his arm, and he had to close his eyes for a moment. "You missed a sense. What about taste?"

Ah. She'd reached the crux of the matter with that simple tease of a question.

"Your mouth haunts me," he told her. "When you bite your lip, my hand slips on the microfilm machine controls, and I zip past weeks' worth of colonial newspapers. I drop my pens. I run into desks and bookshelves, because I'm thinking about how soft and glossy your mouth looks. How you would taste. How much pressure you prefer in a kiss.

Whether you'd squirm a little if I sucked on the tip of your tongue."

She squirmed a bit then, no sucking needed, so he was pretty sure he had his answer to that last question.

"Thomas…" Her hand landed on his knee over the covers, and her gaze was soft and searching. "I don't understand. If you want me so much, why have you been rushing to bed each night and leaving before I wake up?"

He swept a hand, indicating the room. "Because of all this."

Her dark brows beetled. "You don't like our hotel?"

"The hotel is great. So were the others, in their own, extremely unique ways." He took her hand and laced their fingers together. "And let me be clear. I jumped at the chance to spend an entire week with you. This trip has been the greatest windfall of my life, bar none."

She'd stiffened by his side. "But?"

"I think…" How to say it in a way that didn't sound patronizing? "I think it would be very easy for someone on this show to mistake forced proximity for real affection."

She shrank back against the headboard, hurt pinching her face. "You're worried your feelings for me might disappear when we fly home to Virginia?"

Oh, Lord. He was fucking this up via his clumsy attempts at subtlety.

He jettisoned caution and spoke plainly. "Callie, I've wanted you for months, and that's not going to change. I'm not worried that my feelings for you will fade. I'm worried *you* won't want *me* once we get back home. I'm worried about taking advantage of you while you're overwhelmed by the intimacy of the whole situation, and I'm worried I might override any hesitancy you might have because I want you so damn much."

He sighed. "And that's a lot of worrying for a man who

generally doesn't worry, so I wanted to discuss my concerns with you."

Moments of silence ticked past.

Her plump lips had gone thin. "That's patronizing as hell, Thomas."

Shit. He'd been right the first time.

"Let me see if I have this straight. You want to kiss me." In response to her questioning look, he nodded. "But you won't, because you think I don't know my own mind right now. That I might get lost in the process somehow and French you back in a sort of vacation-induced stupor. Is that correct?"

Good thing she wasn't turning that beetle-browed glare to the shore visible outside their window. As he'd noted, the tides would have stilled. Immediately.

Her voice was a lash, and he winced at its sting. "How about if I kiss you instead? Is that acceptable? Or would it be further evidence of my maidenly confusion?"

"Okay, I know what I said sounded stupid and condescending. I get it." He held tight to her hand when she started to slide it free from his. "But Callie, be honest. Can you really tell me you don't have any doubts? That you aren't worried about what might happen when we're back in Marysburg?"

"I worry about everything." She sounded beyond grouchy. "That's not a fair question."

He waited.

Eventually, she sighed. "But yes, maybe I'm a bit concerned about how I can reconcile this"—she squeezed his fingers—"with our work relationship."

"Callie..." Might as well say what he meant. All of it, while he had the chance. "As long as you still have doubts about me and our future together, I don't want to become more intimate. Because if you and I kissed or made love and you regretted it afterward, I don't know how I'd be able to move past that."

It would destroy him. Leave him desolate, the ground salted beneath his feet.

Her voice had turned quiet. Tentative. "When we had to work together, you mean?"

He sighed. "That too."

Finally, she understood him. He could tell by the glaze of shock in those dark eyes.

"You want me that much?" The words vibrated with a kind of emotional intensity he couldn't quite decipher. "You care about me that much?"

"Yes." He stroked the back of her hand with his thumb. "So I need your assistance. Until you're completely, unequivocally sure you'll want to be with me once we return home, please take pity on a besotted former academic. Help me keep a certain amount of distance."

"No one can promise forever," she reminded him.

He acknowledged that with a lift of his shoulder. "Right now, I'm not asking for forever. Just next week."

One side of that lush mouth tilted. "So don't tempt you. And don't kiss you until I'm absolutely certain I won't regret it." Her head inclined a fraction. "I can do that. Or, more accurately, *not* do that."

"Thank you." He nudged her arm with his. "I'm grateful."

"And in return, will you promise to trust me if and when I say I *am* sure?"

Her brows were raised in challenge, and he smoothed each of them with a stroke of his free thumb. "I promise."

"So we're good now? I can eat breakfast, take my anxiety meds, and stop having intense conversations before I've had even a single cup of coffee?"

He laughed. "We're good."

She eased her hand from his and headed for the room's little coffee station.

"Want to see whether the resort is offering a snorkeling cruise this morning? We should have time to do it before we need to make our"—she crooked her fingers—"*big decision*. Especially since Gladys surrendered to our charm offensive and didn't schedule anything specific for this morning."

Callie wanted him to spend several hours staring at her in a wet bathing suit?

Oh, no.

But also: Oh, *yes*.

"Reserve the tickets," he told her, and promptly left the bedroom in search of a cold, cold shower.

CALLIE EYED THE WATER DOWN BELOW, THOSE tempting lips pursed.

The captain of their vessel had zipped to the side of the island that boasted a sunken ship—sunken via holes strategically placed by the island's owners, because they'd wanted a snorkeling feature nearby—and tossed a rope around a cushioned wooden pole sticking out of the clear water. The pole implied the water wasn't too deep in that spot, and there were multiple employees watching out for the safety of all the tourists aboard.

Still, Callie hesitated.

The colorful trim on her goggles almost matched that heart-stopping coral suit she wore, and her flippers fit perfectly. Which Thomas knew, because he'd checked. Her mouthpiece swung from her clenched hand with every restless movement. An inner tube waited for each of them in the rippling waves below, held by another patient crew member, so she wouldn't need to worry about staying afloat once she ventured in the water.

The single cameraman who'd accompanied them to the boat had braced himself against some sort of fiberglass bulwark and was capturing every moment on film, as Gladys had insisted.

Everything was ready. Everything but Callie.

When he laid his hand on her shoulder, the strengthening sun had turned her silky skin feverish. "Do you want to jump in together?"

She cast a dubious glance at the narrow gap in the rail. "There's not room for both of us."

"There is if I hold you." He'd lowered his voice to a whisper, since maybe the crew wouldn't love that idea. But he couldn't come up with another solution that would allow Callie to move past her anxiety and give herself what she wanted. "We'll just have to make sure we jump far enough out from the boat."

She nestled into him, front to front, her arms wrapped around his waist, and he almost whimpered as her breath ghosted against his earlobe. "Not to be rude, but maybe potentially-dangerous feats of physical prowess aren't exactly your greatest gift?"

"I'd never let you get hurt." He might whack himself against the boat on the way down, but she wouldn't get a single scratch. Not while he was alive, conscious, and within arm's reach. "Trust me."

Silence.

Moisture glinted on her lashes as she stared up at him, and she was biting that lower lip.

Dammit. She was going to be so disappointed and angry at herself if they didn't do this, but he wouldn't push her to do anything—anything—that made her uncomfortable.

He frowned. "Sweetheart, we don't have to jump. We can

stay on board, or there's an inclined ladder toward the back of the boat—"

She nodded toward the gap in the rail. "Are you ready?"

He blinked at her. "Of course, but like I said, we don't—"

"I trust you." Her voice was firm. Decisive. "So here we go."

As it turned out, Callie boasted not only surpassing beauty and softness, but also a startling amount of physical strength. Because the next thing he knew, the two of them were flying off the side of the boat, powered only by the might of those curvy legs.

Somehow, they lost hold of one another as they smacked into the water, and as soon as he made his way to the surface and oriented himself, he swung his head in a frantic search for Callie.

The search didn't last long. He just needed to follow her giggles.

"Are you all right?" She reached out a hand and tugged him to her side. "The water's so warm!"

"I'm fine." More than fine, actually. Delighted and proud.

Her legs shifted in a graceful, sinuous kick beneath the water as the nearby crew member handed them their inner tubes.

She hooked an arm around her yellow doughnut, contemplated the opening for a moment, looked down at her chest, and shrugged. "I think I can wedge myself into this thing. Let's find out."

After a couple minutes of fumbling and goggles readjustment, the two of them were floating on the surface, their faces in the water, the inner tubes supporting their middles as they studied the deliberate wreck and the schools of glinting fish darting beneath them.

Callie's fingers had intertwined with his, and he couldn't spot any signs of tension in her movements. Which was why he was startled when she squeezed his hand and suddenly went vertical.

He did the same, only to see her remove her goggles and mouthpiece.

They'd only been snorkeling for a short time, but maybe she'd gotten a cramp? Or started worrying about drifting too far away from the boat?

He yanked off his own goggles and mouthpiece, so he could see her better and speak intelligibly. "Are you o—"

Her free hand curled around the back of his neck and guided him closer, despite the hindrance of the inner tubes. Then closer, until all he could smell was salt and Callie. The goggles had drawn a faint line on her forehead, her hair sleeked against her head in a shining cap, and her tongue—

Her tongue, unless he was mistaken, had just licked a drop of water from his ear.

The nearby tourists, the boat, the ocean itself ceased to exist.

"I can't wait any longer." Her fingers threaded through his hair and cupped his skull. "I'm sure, Thomas. So you need to trust *me*."

Her lips pressed to his, soft as velvet and warm as the sun on his back.

It was loving affirmation in kiss form, neither hurried nor demanding. When his hand cupped her cheek, she nestled against the touch with a sigh he breathed into his lungs, and that cool cheek heated beneath his fingers as her mouth opened to his tongue.

She tasted of salt and sweetness, and she smiled when he rumbled a desperate surrender of a groan into that tempting mouth. When he wrenched himself away to explore further, she grasped him with trembling fingers, trying to draw him back to her lips as he trailed a path from her lips to her jaw and licked that fragrant, shadowy spot just below her ear.

Musk and roses. Delicious.

She moaned, and he surged upward to capture it against his tongue.

The kiss stretched into the entirety of the ocean, and when they paused for a moment, both breathing in rapid rasps, she whispered his name with such longing he nearly floated away.

Then he blinked his eyes open and realized: They *were* floating away.

The gentle current had inexorably nudged them farther from the other tourists. The captain appeared to be saying something into a megaphone and waving them back toward the ship with a certain amount of controlled impatience, as if she'd been doing it for a while. A crew member was swimming in their direction. And Thomas's hands were empty of everything but Callie.

Callie smoothed back the hair plastered against his forehead and gifted him with one last, lingering brush of her mouth against his. A tender, private caress, despite the watchful eye of HATV's camera lens.

Then she smiled at him. "Let's go find your goggles and mouthpiece, shall we?"

He was hers. She'd claimed him.

What else could he do but follow?

SEVEN

"OH, MY GOD, TESS." CALLIE LEANED INTO THE mirror and smoothed on a thin layer of makeup primer. "Thank you for telling me about Renaissance Island. This place is so relaxing. Yesterday afternoon, a dude named Sven pummeled me into massage-drunk jelly, and the snorkeling trip this morning was incredible. The water's so clear and warm and calm it's like a baby's bath."

Her cell was resting on the bathroom vanity, the speaker activated so she could continue getting ready for the upcoming sit-down interview, where she and Thomas would discuss the three island options and end all faux-suspense by choosing one of them for the rest of the trip.

"I know, right?" Tess gave a rueful laugh. "Although I have to admit, I probably spent more time on the tennis courts than on the beach."

"The beaches are gorgeous, but Thomas and I met Lucas just before dinner last night." Callie said, carefully mixing a squirt of her foundation with a dollop of moisturizer on the back of her hand. "I can safely say you made the right decision. Damn, woman."

Lucas was a tall drink of twenty-something hotness, and no one could blame Tess for gulping him down. Even better: When Callie had mentioned her friend's name, his face had softened and lit in a way that was almost painful to witness.

He clearly adored Tess. Enough that he was finishing out his contract with the resort and planning a move to Maryland. So yeah, Callie had approved of him. Wholeheartedly.

"Is Thomas there with you right now?" Tess sounded cautious. "Or can you talk freely?"

After showering, dressing in the bathroom, and giving her a tender, sweet buss on her temple, he'd gone out to get them a belated breakfast from the little café on the first floor. Given his usual speed of decision-making and movement, she figured she had plenty of time to chat.

"He's grabbing food." She sponged the foundation mixture over her face and neck, blending the edges thoroughly into her skin until no line of demarcation remained. "And that brings me to the other reason I owe you a big thank-you. He and I are together now. Like, boyfriend-and-girlfriend, drawing-hearts-in-the-sand-with-our-initials-inside together."

A long pause. "What?"

Callie loaded up her little highlighter brush. "I said, Thomas and I are dating now, and I'm so grateful you convinced me to come here. Thank you."

Another, longer pause. "Are you joking?"

"No." Tess hit the inner corners of her eyes and her cheekbones.

Total silence.

"Honey, I have time, but not all day." No need for blush, not after how the sun and water had conquered her sunscreen that morning. "Whatever you want to say, spit it out."

"Callie…" Her friend spoke slowly. "You hate Thomas."

She frowned down at the phone. Eye makeup would have to wait.

"No, I don't," she said.

"Uh, yeah." Tess didn't sound combative. More befuddled. "Yeah, you do."

"I don't think I ever hated him. Not really." She'd been thinking about that over the past few days. A lot. "I've had a hard couple of years, and changing jobs is really stressful. Not to mention how bad things got with Andre in the end. I think I was looking for a scapegoat, and Thomas served that purpose."

She flicked on the water to wash some stray highlighter from her fingers, and the plumbing made an odd sort of *thunk*.

"I hear what you're saying." Tess's words almost dripped with doubt. "But Cal, during almost every conversation we've had over the past four months, you've either raged or cried about how he's screwing you over at the library. Because of him, you've spent your workdays stressed to the point where you might as well buy stock in anti-anxiety meds."

Callie bit her lip and stared down into the sink, rinsing away the soap and letting the cool water rush over her wrists. Sometimes that trick helped calm her when she got overwhelmed, and sometimes it didn't. But it was worth a try.

Tess wasn't finished. "Those complaints weren't the product of any frustration and loneliness you were experiencing in other areas of your life. Andre didn't somehow make certain you never had a moment to breathe on the desk, and job transition stress didn't ensure you were always scheduled alongside Thomas. One man caused those problems, Cal. One man. Thomas. I can't count how many times you told me you couldn't stand to see his face behind the desk. That you loathed working with him."

Swallowing over such a dry throat hurt.

"And after three days sharing a hotel room, you're apparently dating the man. So please forgive me if I'm a bit confused and concerned." Tess's Vice Principal Voice softened and lowered. "I don't want you hurt. I don't like the idea of someone taking advantage of a fraught situation to get closer to you. And I don't see how you could make a relationship with him work when you want to rip out his throat after every shift together."

At that, Callie's spine stiffened, and she turned off the water. Which made a weird thump again, but whatever. They could call maintenance later.

"He didn't take advantage of me." When Tess started to say something, Callie overrode her. "I mean it. He didn't even want to kiss me during this trip, because he wanted to be absolutely sure our circumstances weren't responsible for my attraction to him."

"Well, I guess that's something," Tess muttered.

"And he doesn't mean any harm at work. He just doesn't multitask well, and I don't know if he could change that even if he wanted to." Callie drummed an eyeliner pencil against the vanity. "I understand him better now, so I don't think I'll get as frustrated as I used to."

"Okay." Tess didn't sound convinced.

To be fair, the argument did sound a bit weak when spoken aloud.

Callie checked the time on her phone display and gave a little, panicked shriek. "Oh, shit. I need to go, Tess. We'll talk later, all right?"

"Sounds good." Her friend hesitated. "Just...take good care of yourself, sweetie. Please."

Callie couldn't help but smile, despite the renewed worries crowding her mind. "Such a mother hen."

They said goodbye, and Callie tried to concentrate on

finishing her eye makeup. Just after she emerged from the bathroom, a loud knock sounded at the door.

She looked through the peephole. Good Lord, had Thomas lost his keycard again?

"You're a mess, McKinney. We need to clip your card to your pocket somehow," she said as she opened the door. "Do you remember where you last saw it?"

Thomas didn't answer, and he didn't come inside the room.

Instead, he handed her one of two paper bags and glanced down at the subtle swirls of the carpet. His mouth opened, but he pressed it shut again.

Oh, no. She'd hurt his feelings.

She laid a hand on his cheek, still smooth from his morning shave. It was hot beneath her palm, brushed with hectic color as if he too had stayed out in the sun too long. "I was just teasing, Thomas. You're not a mess. People lose their keycards all the time. If you need another one, we'll get it. And I don't mind keeping mine handy for the both of us."

He stepped back from the contact, and her hand fell to her side.

"I'll give you some privacy to keep getting ready." He was so quiet, she could barely hear him. "Take your time, and I'll meet you and the crew in the lobby."

When he finally met her eyes, he offered her a smile.

It was weak and fleeting and not at all like Thomas, and she felt like a monster.

Oh, God, they were going to have to talk about this, weren't they? "But—"

She'd waited too long.

"But I am ready," she told the closed door.

CALLIE HAD LOATHED HIM.

Loathed him.

All those months on the desk, Thomas had thought she'd grown distant because of difficulties with Andre or her family or something else in her private life.

But no. She'd distanced herself from him because she couldn't stand the sight of his face. Because he made her cry, rage, and become anxious.

Even before this trip, he'd thought they were friends of a sort. And while he'd wanted much, much more than that, he'd taken comfort in having any type of relationship with such an amazing woman. But the entire time, he'd been making her life harder, making her miserable, and making her hate him.

In a far corner of the sunshine-hued lobby, an armchair lurked behind the fronds of a potted bush. He sank into its cushion and covered his face with shaking hands.

Every shift they'd spent together for the past four months, he'd orchestrated. Timed his schedule requests so he could be near her as often as possible, without ever thinking about whether that was what *she* wanted. And then, during those shifts, he'd tried his best to block her out so he could concentrate on patron questions, just as he did with all his other coworkers.

The only difference: She'd never left his mind. Not entirely.

But fumbling pencils when she bit her lip or admiring her efficiency at locating the exact right journal article for a patron wasn't the same thing as actually paying attention to her.

Not as his fantasy, the object of his desire. But as Callie Adesso, a subject in her own right, with wants and needs and goals at work that might not match his own.

Did all his other coworkers secretly hate working with him too? Did they sigh with relief every time they glanced at the schedule and saw that, once again, Callie would serve as the sacrificial librarian for the entire department?

She never worked with any of the others, not given the schedule Thomas ensured for her. Had that—had *he*—stopped her from making closer ties at the library? Was he the reason she never went to the bar with them anymore, or to dinner after the library closed?

He could envision her standing behind the desk, facing an onslaught of patrons alone. How many times had he registered that sight in a distracted glance, and then turned back to his own work without offering a single bit of help?

So many lines. She'd dispatched so many lines of people with seeming ease, with seeming happiness, but thinking back, he could recognize that tight smile. That glassy stare. That veneer of calm and professionalism hiding profound anxiety.

He'd believed the mask.

No, that was offering him too much credit.

He hadn't even bothered to question it.

Should he leave the library? But what in the world could he possibly do instead? Several years as an adjunct professor at Marysburg University and multiple failed bids for tenure-track jobs had proven him entirely too scattered, too unambitious, and too slow for a life in academia. Teaching at a public school, from what he'd heard, would require even more efficiency. And if he tried to lead tours through the historic area, they'd probably last a decade each.

What other people think, what they might expect or want from me, doesn't concern me, he'd told Callie yesterday. And he'd done so with...

Not pride. Not exactly. But total acceptance. An assumption that he couldn't and didn't need to change that about himself. That his obliviousness was, at worst, a harmless character quirk. When all the while he'd been hurting the woman he loved, and maybe all his other coworkers too.

The shame of it. He'd never experienced anything like the shame that burned his cheeks and shuddered through his body and roiled his stomach.

That shame and a terrible, grinding grief had nearly brought him to his knees just inside the hotel room door, listening to her phone conversation over the sound of running water.

He'd lost her. Lost her, before he even truly had her.

Because how could he possibly believe Callie wanted a future with him?

Every time they worked together, she'd remember what he'd done to her. How oblivious he'd been to her needs and desires. How could she ever trust him?

And how could he possibly assume this change of heart, her profession of interest, was anything but the psychological effect of days spent in the same bed, in the same space, pretending to be in love on camera? A cable-television, tropical version of Stockholm Syndrome?

He couldn't.

He couldn't.

Confrontations and awkward, emotionally fraught discussions made her anxious. Gave her hives. So he wasn't going to inflict one on her, because he was done hurting Callie Adesso.

Instead, he'd fake a smile for this last on-camera interview, wave off the HATV crew, and leave her the hell alone. Let her enjoy her vacation and recover from the stress he'd inflicted on her for months. Talk to their supervisor and try to change his schedule as soon as they returned home.

And he'd do it even through this tearing ache in his chest. For her. For Callie, the woman he loved.

Because avoiding her, he finally understood, was the best way to show that love.

EIGHT

Thomas didn't touch her the rest of the day. Not once.

They'd endured their final interminable interview in yet another generic hotel meeting room. They'd discussed the benefits and drawbacks of different islands and announced their decision to stay their last three nights on Renaissance Island. The crew had contacted the other hotels and a ferry company to cancel reservations. She and Thomas had made their goodbyes to the crew and seen everyone off at the ferry dock.

All the while, he hadn't once reached for her hand or wrapped an arm around her waist or stroked the wind-whipped hair from her face. All gestures she'd apparently become dependent on during the course of three short days, because their absence hurt.

More than that, their absence confused her.

Because he still smiled at her, the expression weaker than normal but seemingly sincere. He saw to her comfort, such as when he'd noticed her shifting in that too-narrow chair with the wooden arms and brought her a wider seat without a word. He'd backed up whatever opinions she expressed during the interview and deflected Gladys's occasional complaints about the lack of great footage on Renaissance Island.

And if she'd truly hurt his feelings so badly with one insensitive remark, why didn't he tell her so? Why didn't he initiate another one of those nerve-wracking conversations of his? Why didn't he share what he was thinking, as he— unlike her—had seemed to do so ably and comfortably before now?

Maybe he'd been waiting for the crew to leave?

But when the ferry disappeared over the horizon, he spoke without looking at her.

"You probably want to sit in the water and relax for a while." His eyes didn't crinkle at the corners, despite his smile. "Don't worry about entertaining me. I found a few local history books, and I might take a tour of the grounds to locate some of the landmarks."

From the sharp pain and coppery taste on her tongue, she must have broken the skin of her lip as she bit it. "Okay."

She didn't expect him to spend every minute with her, of course, but...

Yeah. It stung. And something was clearly amiss.

Say something, Cal. She shifted on feet that had suddenly started to hurt, pinched by her strappy sandals. *For Christ's sake, take his hand and ask what happened. Ask him what's wrong.*

But the thought of that tripped her heart in her chest and made her skin prickle with both humiliation and hives. She couldn't do it. Not when his answer meant so much to her, and the wrong response could crush her.

Maybe he simply needed some alone time, away from her incessant worries, and was too kind to tell her that outright. If so, she couldn't exactly blame him. And if she forced him to stay with her, to have that awkward, potentially hurtful conversation, maybe he'd get angry. Maybe he'd think she was too demanding, too needy.

Maybe he'd tell her they were through. That she was too much for him.

No, she should let him go. Let him work through his thoughts and come back to her. If he had something he needed to tell her, he would. In his own time. She wouldn't force the issue.

His blue eyes had turned dull. Opaque. "I hope you have an amazing day, Callie."

Her chest was afire, her throat thick. She didn't want him to see her in this state. So when he turned to leave, she didn't call him back.

She did what she always did. What she did best.

She kept her mouth shut and put one foot in front of the other, no matter how much it hurt.

LATE THAT AFTERNOON, SHE SENT HIM A TEXT. *JUST a reminder: We have reservations for dinner at seven. Meet you in our room before then.*

Then she shut down her phone before he could text back to cancel. Because if she knew Thomas—and she did, or at least she'd *thought* she did—if she didn't confirm that she'd received his message, he'd show up to their room out of sheer politeness.

And she needed to see him. To reassure herself that every-thing hadn't gone wrong, much as she knew it had. Suddenly. For reasons she feared she comprehended all too well.

True to form, he arrived in their suite half an hour before the reservation, and his eyes immediately flew to the corner of the room where she sat, fully dressed and ready to go.

"Hello, Callie." He cleared his throat. "Did you have a good afternoon?"

She could interpret the wince creasing his lean face. He'd wanted to cancel, but only a jackass would do so at the last minute, when she'd clearly spent time and effort preparing for the occasion.

Oh, yes, she knew him. Not as well as she'd hoped, but well enough to stage this moment. Now she just had to figure out what to do with it.

He didn't come within five feet of her, and he didn't make eye contact as he scuttled around the room and gathered clothing for a dinner that would undoubtedly be horrible and stilted.

She was wearing her goddess dress again, and he didn't even give her a second glance.

So much for Amazon queens. She should have known better.

And at that moment, something broke inside her.

Fuck her anxiety. Fuck her hives. She had things to say to Thomas McKinney, and he was going to listen, like it or not.

"No." This time, the voice that emerged from her mouth wasn't tentative, Anxious Callie Voice. It wasn't even smooth, competent, Professional Librarian Voice. This one was new. Loud. If she had to give it a name, she thought she might call it Callie's Had Enough of This Shit Voice. "No, I didn't have a good afternoon. I'd thank you for asking, but since you're the cause of my crappy day, I think I'll forgo that pro forma response."

He spun to face her, that firm jaw going slightly slack.

She sat forward in her chair. "I don't know what the hell happened this morning. I'm sorry I called you a mess, but I already apologized for that, and I did so sincerely. If you're still angry about it, we can talk it over, but I don't think what I said was unforgivable."

"It's not—" His words stuttered to a halt. "Callie, no, that's not—"

"But I suspect that's not the problem at all. Maybe once the cameras were about to leave, you realized you'd gotten swept up in this whole experience, and you started considering everything you've learned about me these past three days. Maybe you finally realized being with me would be an enormous pain in your ass, and you don't want to hurt my feelings by saying so." She rose to her feet. "But now's your chance. I'm topped up on Benadryl, so do your worst. Tell me why you don't want to look at me or touch me anymore, despite everything you said j-just"—her voice wavered—"this morning. Tell me I'm too needy or too anxious. Tell me I'm too much for you."

Her breath hitched, but she refused to scratch at her hive-ridden chest.

His eyes had closed with her words, his face scrunched into an expression of pain she understood. He was a good man, and he didn't want to hurt her feelings.

But she was going to force him to do it, because she was done being silent and wondering what might have been different if she'd only said something. Advocated for herself. Asked questions and clarified what was happening in her world.

If he was going to dump her abruptly, she was damn well going to know why.

When his eyes opened again, she jerked in shock.

They weren't opaque anymore. They were wet, like hers.

But he didn't reach for her or move closer.

"I know, Callie." The words were choked. "I *know*."

She threw her hands in the air, infuriated and befuddled. "What does that even *mean*?"

Her heart drummed through several beats of silence.

"I—" His deep breath lifted and lowered his chest. "I

came back with breakfast this morning, and you were in the bathroom. I overheard your conversation with your friend."

What?

Oh.

Oh, shit.

"Thomas." She took a step toward him. "How much did you hear?"

"I'm so sorry." His shoulders slumped, and he gazed down at his sneakers. "I shouldn't have listened to a private conversation. But most of all, I'm sorry for making you so miserable. I'm sorry I didn't realize how much I was hurting you. I'm sorry you thought for even a moment I considered you too much. And I'm sorry that because of me, you're forcing yourself to have another awkward conversation that's giving you hives."

The defeat in his voice tore at her heart.

"The hives don't matter. I have medication to help with that." She exhaled through her nose and took another step toward him. "If you heard everything, then you know I've changed my—"

He backed away, toward the door. "I don't know how to make this right. But clearly there's no way we can have a future together. So I figure the best thing I can do for you is let you have a relaxing vacation and talk to Bridget about our schedule as soon as we get back. I promise I'll try to avoid you in the future. But if that's not enough, let me know, and I'll see whether I can find somewhere else to work. Maybe a research library in Plymouth."

What? What the hell was he talking about?

He lifted his hand in what was likely meant to be a sort of sad farewell gesture, and she actually stomped her foot.

No. She wasn't letting him duck out of this conversation until she understood everything.

"If you want to make this right, you'll stop moving toward

the door and answer my goddamn question." She pinned him with her glare. "How much did you *hear*?"

He was staring at her brows, seemingly frozen. If she hadn't been so upset, she probably would have laughed.

"Thomas?" she prompted.

He visibly started. "Uh…your friend said you loathed me. Because I always scheduled myself with you and left you stranded on the desk. Which is true, and like I said, I'm so sorry, Callie. I wish with every cell in my body I could go back six months and do everything differently, but I can't."

"And you didn't hear my response?"

He shook his head. "I left before that. Then I gave you enough time to finish your conversation before coming back."

If they had any chance of moving past this, they needed to lance the wound. So she pointed to the bed. "You obviously didn't hear everything. But let's talk about what you did hear for a minute. Take a seat."

"Okay." He shuffled across the room and settled on the edge of the mattress, his eyes pained and resigned. "If you want to have this conversation, I'm ready to listen."

Where to start? After months of frustration and days of affection, where to start?

"Do you deliberately match your schedule requests to mine every month?" At his nod, she sank back into the chair. "You should've asked me before doing that, Thomas. I never get the chance to work closely with anyone else, which isolates me at the library. And more importantly, it isn't your right to control my life that way."

"I know." He sat perfectly still and held her gaze, not a hint of denial or anger on that pale, grief-creased face. "I'm so, so sorry."

"Will you do it again without asking me first?"

"No." He shook his head violently. "God, no."

"Then on to the next issue. You need to give me the opportunity to deal with more complex questions. Without them, I can't prove my worth to the library or use my training and academic background." She waited for his nod. "And you have to pay more attention to what's happening around you while you're working. If there's a long line, tell people you'll get back to them later. Research on the eighteenth century isn't a life-or-death situation, and it can wait an hour, or even a day or two. Other patrons are important too. So are your coworkers."

"I understand what you're saying. I'm not…" He hung his head. "I'm not great at multitasking, but I'll try. I swear to God, Callie, I'll try harder."

The desolation on his face twisted her heart, but she took a gulp of air and forced herself to finish. "Last thing. I know I need to stop measuring myself against other people's opinions and expectations all the time. But you need to do it more often. Because self-confidence is great, but obliviousness isn't."

He flinched, but he met her eyes. "I've thought about this all day, and I agree. Completely."

"Then I'm done." She let out a slow breath. "That's all I have to say about work."

Maybe she was still itchy, but her head felt so light it could almost float away.

She'd done it.

She'd laid out every single point she'd mentally screamed at him for months. She'd done so clearly and succinctly, and she'd made herself understood.

He'd listened. Of course he'd listened. But more than that, he *got it*, he didn't appear to hate her for what she'd said, and he was going to try to do better.

With their past tackled, it was time to look to their future. Together.

"Again, I'm so sorry." He'd risen to his feet, and he took a step toward the door once more. "I wish I'd paid more attention months ago, but I'll do better in the future. I promise you'll never have to deal with my bullshit again. But please know that I never, ever wanted to hurt you. You deserve the world, and I…"

His words grew reedy and hoarse. "I wish I were a man you could love. But whoever he is, he'll be the luckiest man ever to draw breath on this Earth."

He offered her one last sweet, sad smile. His eyes glowed with that unshadowed adoration she'd seen just that morning, and they lovingly traced every feature of her face. Like she'd fallen from the heavens, his heart's desire in flesh. Beautiful but too divine to touch.

And then he was walking toward that damn door again.

Really? *Really?*

"Thomas?"

He let go of the door handle and looked over his shoulder at her.

She raised her brows. "Aren't you forgetting something?"

Patting his pocket, he frowned. "I have my keycard. And I'll reserve my own room before tonight, so don't worry. I'll pack while you're at dinner."

Jesus Christ.

"I didn't mean your keycard." She waited for a moment, but he simply continued to stare at her. "I mean, weren't you supposed to *ask* me what I wanted from now on?"

"Oh." He hesitated. "Did you want to move to a different room, instead of me? I figured it would be easier for you if—"

If she murdered him, any jury would consider it justifiable homicide.

"*No.*" When she walked up to him and gripped the front of his tee in a fist, he blinked down at her, his eyes wide. "I want you to ask me how I feel about you. How I want our future to look. Instead of assuming what I want and how I feel *once again*."

Okay, so maybe she raised her voice a bit. Again, justifiable.

Against her knuckles, the rapid tattoo of his heartbeat told her everything. And even if it hadn't, the way he stopped breathing would have.

He gazed down at her, the grief in his eyes turning to shock. Tentative hope.

"How—" He gulped. "How do you feel about me? How do you want our future to look?"

The words were wisps of noise, vibrating with emotion.

"I like you." She loosened her fingers and smoothed the wrinkled cotton of his tee, then spread her hand flat against his chest. "Given more time, I think I could love you. I already love your curiosity and intelligence. I already love your sincerity. I already love how you focus on me so completely and listen with such wholehearted attention. I already love your good intentions and your willingness to admit when you're wrong. I already love your protectiveness and your wry sense of humor. And despite its drawbacks, I even love your ability to accept who you are." She smiled up at him. "Which, as you know, is not my forte."

"You don't want me to be"—he cringed a bit—"different?"

"Only in the ways we've already discussed." She stroked her hand up to his shoulder and watched him shiver beneath her touch. "And it's not as if I don't have things to work on too. If I'm angry or frustrated or disappointed, I need to make myself talk about it, not just stew in silence for months at a time. Even if it's awkward and causes hives. If you'd known my concerns earlier, would you have done something about them? Would you have changed the way you work?"

He covered her hand with his. "I would have done my damnedest, Callie. I swear."

"So what happened wasn't all your fault." Her head fit perfectly into the crook of his neck, and he smelled grassy and delicious. "Especially since, as I told Tess, I think part of my rage and anxiety had nothing to do with you. I spent three years working a full-time job and taking classes at the same time, so my levels of stress coming into the library were already off the charts. And for someone like me, changing jobs is destabilizing. When you add a failing relationship to that mix, I had a lot of emotions looking for a convenient home, and there you were. Happily working away at the microfilm machine while I helped three dozen impatient colonial people."

He gently tipped up her chin to look her in the eye. "You were right to be angry at me, Callie."

She ducked her head to kiss his hand. "Yes, I was. But maybe not quite as angry as I actually was. And this afternoon, something else occurred to me."

With his thumb, he stroked her jaw. "What's that?"

"We got so close so fast when I started working at CMRL. Maybe too close, for someone dating another man." When he pursed his lips in understanding, she nodded. "Yeah. I think all that anger was a good way to keep you at a distance while my relationship with Andre played out and reached its inevitable, dismal conclusion."

"That makes sense." He pressed a bit closer, his thighs brushing against the folds of her skirt. "Although like I said, I deserved your anger. And I want to make sure you understand something else."

Oh, that glide of his leg against hers felt like fire. "What's that?"

"You're not—and never have been—a pain in my ass." His voice was as steely as she'd ever heard it. Entirely unamused. "Yes, you have needs, but that doesn't make you needy. And

I've always, always wanted more of you, so I don't see you how you could possibly consider yourself too much for me."

"With my anxiety, I'm not..." She shifted her weight. "I'm not always easy."

To her shock, he laughed. "Sweetheart, when did I ever give you the impression I wanted easy?"

He hadn't.

He'd always wanted her for who she was, not who she expected herself to be.

"Never." Her nose tingled, and she blinked away the spangled haze in her vision. "Never, Thomas."

His lean frame radiated heat, and the muscles of his arm tensed beneath her trailing fingers. The thumb at her jaw shifted, drifting down her neck and to her shoulder in a gentle, heated path. Then it halted, and he swallowed hard.

"Callie, I need to do this right, so let me be clear." He cupped her face, his fingers light and careful. "I want you. In my life, in my bed, in my heart. Do you want me?"

She beamed a smile. "Yup."

His eyes flared, and he leaned down until his forehead rested against hers. "So what do you want to do now?"

"Dinner. Beach. Bed." She arched her back until her lower body pressed to his, and that little sound from the back of his throat shot through her in a bolt. "Are you with me?"

He rubbed her nose with his so softly, despite the heated hardness she felt against her belly. "Always."

NINE

"THIS IS OUR SPOT." CALLIE LAID HER TOWEL ON AN empty two-person lounger and smiled at Thomas. "What do you think?"

He had his hands on his hips, his eyes to the endless waters on the horizon. "It's beautiful here. Just like your friend said."

In fact, Tess had said more. "Almost no one goes there," she'd told Callie before the trip. "It's a secluded spot, kids aren't allowed, and most adults don't want to walk so far from the hotel. If you want time to yourself, that's the place."

Tess hadn't lied. This section of the beach was deserted. Especially late at night.

No kids burying their parents in sand. No other couples wading hand-in-hand through the surf. No one floating on the ubiquitous sunshine-yellow rafts supplied by the resort. No producers or camera operators or boom mic guys. Not even a single hair-and-makeup woman lamenting the shiny state of Callie's T-zone.

She and Thomas had finally, finally found a spot where they could be completely alone. A miraculous, adults-only stretch of moonlit sand, cushioned loungers, and dark, lazy waves, the rustling palm fronds above the flawless accompaniment to a spectacular, humid evening.

Perfect for her purposes.

A little bit more foreplay. One last tease of a taste before the feast.

"Do you want to sit in the water?" Thomas smoothed a stray strand of hair back from her temple, then cupped the nape of her neck with his long, warm fingers. "Or lie down for a while under the palms?"

He'd listened. Listened and remembered. And as always, no one could mistake the adoration and gentleness in his hands.

He was totally getting lucky that night.

"Let's share this lounger." She sat on its low edge, sliding away from his touch. "I think we could both use a little rest."

His mouth opened, but he pressed it shut again. And his eyes were now glued to the wide chair, roaming from corner to corner as if he were doing some mental math.

He could save himself the effort. She'd already run the calculations, and there was no way they could both fit on that thing without entwining their bodies in a hot tangle.

His fingers curled into his palms.

She patted the cushion invitingly.

"Callie, is this really the place you want to—"

His voice choked into silence. Probably because he'd finally looked down at her and noticed her face's proximity to a very specific part of his plaid swim trunks.

When she rose to her feet again, she deliberately brushed up against him, and he staggered way more than necessary in response to such light contact. Then she moved a few steps away—to offer him a better view—grasped the hem of her gauzy sundress with both hands, tugged it over her head, and dropped it on the sand.

After dinner, she'd changed into a one-piece swimsuit the color of whipped cream, with thin shoulder straps dropping into a deep vee in front. The design—her favorite among the suits she'd brought—left her back almost completely bare, down to the incipient swells of her ass. And a good chunk of that ass was exposed by high-leg cut.

It was a death blow to his control, delivered in swimsuit form. Or so she hoped.

Thomas gaped at her for a moment, then squeezed his eyes shut, the flush on his handsome face evident even in near-darkness, his toes curling in the sand.

Some women her size wouldn't dare wear a suit like that, no matter how much it flattered them. Wouldn't leave themselves unprotected from the judgment of people who might whisper to their friends that big girls like her should know better than to reveal so much flesh in public; that big girls like her should be ashamed and hidden, always.

She knew what it felt like to feel uncomfortable and embarrassed. God, did she know.

But while countless things made Callie nervous, her body wasn't one of them.

She loved how she looked. Always had, always would. And Thomas felt the same way. He'd never tried to hide that. He couldn't even if he did try.

He was breathing so hard through his nose that his nostrils flared. Those long fingers had formed full-on fists at his sides. And not to be indelicate, but his swim trunks didn't exactly hide his reaction to her.

When she strutted back to him, his eyes opened, but not completely. They were heavy-lidded, as if he were ready for that rest she'd mentioned. But the eyes of a half-asleep man didn't turn incandescent with heat and focus so fiercely on what stood in front of them.

He lifted a single fingertip and laid it on the curve of her shoulder, where the strap bit into her skin. As he watched with rapt attention, that finger descended slowly, tracing the neckline of the suit. The edge of her collarbone leading to the swell of her breast and the shadow of her cleavage. Then up again, each inch of progress deliberate and unhurried as he turned her flesh to fire.

At her other shoulder, he brushed his thumb in a lazy arc over her gooseflesh.

Then he laid his palm over her heart. His hand lingered there without moving for several suspended seconds, and she swayed with her sudden understanding.

He was feeling her heartbeat. Measuring it. Learning it.

Her eyes flooded with happy, humbled tears, and she couldn't stand it anymore. She had to touch him. And she knew exactly where to begin.

She moved the final step forward, took hold of his hips, and tugged him until they were standing pressed together from chest to knees. Those dark curls at his neck had tempted her for way too long, so she buried her fingers in them. Tugged lightly and gloried in his harsh intake of air, the immediate response pressing into her belly.

She rose on tiptoe and whispered in his ear. "If you don't think you can stop at a kiss or two, let's go back to the room."

When he swallowed, she could see the agitated movement of his throat.

"Yes." That low, calm, amused voice had become a rasp. A hoarse gulp of sound.

As soon as she scooped her clothing from the sand, he claimed her other hand and laced their fingers together. She didn't bother donning the sundress again. She didn't mind walking through the hotel in her swimsuit, and she was in a hurry. They both were.

Thomas took the lead, and his long legs ate up the

distance to the hotel. He guided her firmly toward the main elevator, heedless of any onlookers. But at the ding of the opening door, she took control, tugging him inside and backing him against one of those mirrored walls.

At that, he smiled at her in an entirely unfamiliar way. Not kind and patient. Predatory. With fingers spread wide, he stroked her bare back from nape to hip, the sweep of his hand slow and deliberate as he watched her mouth.

She yanked him down to her, and their lips met in a kiss that went nuclear within moments, devouring and hard and wet, as his fingers flexed into her ass, grinding her against him.

Once the elevator arrived at their floor, they raced to their door, breathing harder than justified by the short journey. His fingers gripped hers with almost painful tightness, as if intent to prevent her escape.

Then they'd reached their room. She opened the door and strode inside, impatient for the weight of his body above hers, the claiming stroke of his fingers between her legs, the delicious stretch as he pushed inside her.

No turned backs tonight.

No opposite sides of the bed.

Nothing but her and Thomas, alone, drowning in desire and naked flesh.

Thank God.

CALLIE, NAKED AND SPREAD ACROSS THE BED, struck the words from Thomas's tongue.

Which was unfortunate, because he wanted to tell her that the moon, milky-bright though it was, might have been a shadow compared to her bright glow. He needed to explain the glory of her dark nipples and curved stomach and splayed, velvety arms. He should expound on the profound temptation of rosy, glistening flesh between her ample thighs and praise her unabashed, confident sensuality.

Instead, he stood by the bed, newly naked himself, and basked in her beauty.

When she raised those soft, strong arms to him, though, he found words again. Not poetic ones, but the ones he needed. The right ones.

He crawled to her on the bed, as befitted an acolyte to a goddess, and knelt between her legs. "Sweetheart, what do you want?"

Her lips curved, and her bittersweet eyes melted into pure warmth. "You above me. Part of me. That's all."

He could give her that. And in doing so, ease his own months of hunger.

He descended into her arms and took her mouth, and her plush lips opened to him, all sweetness and bold need. She claimed his tongue, and he shuddered. Then sucked the tip of hers so he could feel the shift of her hips beneath him, could trace the arch of her neck with his fingertips.

Her hands glided down his flanks, his ass, with a hum of praise, but his body meant nothing, nothing, except in service to her. So he concentrated on her and her alone, rather than his own fierce arousal.

He heard the rush of her exhalation when he nipped at the side of her neck, the muscle of her shoulder, the tender curve of her earlobe. Marked the widening welcome of her thighs as he teased those sensitive nipples to tightness with careful strokes of his thumb and the lightest, gentlest pinches. Inhaled her whimper when his hand coasted over her belly and down to the dark, fragrant center of her, where she was plump and unfurling for him like a bloom.

Her clitoris pushed against his thumb as it grew stiff, and her slickness bathed his fingers as he breached her inner softness and found a slow, caressing rhythm that drew her knees tight against his sides.

He wanted to taste her. Pull her atop him and drown in her scent, her response, her thighs around his ears a shelter from the outside world. But more than that, he wanted the sight of her mercurial, expressive face suffused with need, with ecstasy, with—finally—languid satisfaction.

And she'd asked to have him above her, and he would deny her nothing.

He'd buried his face in the curve of her neck to lick and suck as her breaths turned to pants and her flesh started to tremble beneath his touch. But when she began to rock against his thumb, spear herself on his fingers, her cries choked and keening, he raised his head to watch.

She came in unselfconscious abandon, her mouth parted in a long moan, her eyes shut tightly. Her orgasm squeezed his fingers and pulsed through her sex as he gentled his strokes and saw her through the pleasure.

Her neck was damp, vibrating with her heartbeat, when he returned his face there.

She tasted like sweat and roses, and when he traced her face with his fingers, the curve of her mouth humbled him. He'd pleased her. Callie. His Callie.

After a minute, the last traces of her climax faded, and he tenderly cupped her sex.

He needed guidance. "What do you want now?"

She answered immediately, and her whisper was a tickle that speared to his groin. "For you to lose control."

He lifted his head in a jerk and met her heavy-lidded eyes.

"Show me everything in here." She smoothed a hand over his chest, over his heart. "And here. I want all of you."

Her fingers slid down, down, down, and squeezed his cock tight.

He reared to his knees and reached for the bedside table,

where the condom package sat open and waiting. She brushed his hand aside and rolled it down his length with a pleased murmur, and then she opened her legs wide, her knees high.

He took her invitation. He took her.

With the first push of his body into hers, she moaned again and dug those shiny nails into his back, and he felt each one like a spur. He bucked against her, into her, his fingers digging into her hips, her ass, her shoulders in a search for more leverage, more depth.

Dimly, he registered his own muffled, raspy grunts and groans, the rapid rhythm of penetration and withdrawal as he sank again and again into her sleek wetness. And while he hadn't intended to abandon finesse in this way, to treat with her anything but gentleness, she'd asked him to show her his need, his love, and she was responding to its violence, meeting it with her own.

With each impact of his hips against her spread thighs, she ground against him and exhaled a whimpering gasp, and the clutch of her body became tighter and tighter. She began to quiver around his cock, and he braced himself on an arm, his hand sinking deep into the mattress, lifting to watch the push of his body inside hers, the way she jerked and panted when his fingers found her clit and stroked.

This time, she cried out his name as she came. He took that cry into his mouth, then pushed deep one, two, three more times and shouted out his gratitude. His adulation. His reverence, despite all the savagery of his need.

Afterward, he laid in her arms, surrounded by her in every possible way, and he willed the sensation to soak into every molecule of his body, every synapse in his brain, so he'd never lose it.

Those time-travelers would have to fight him for Callie, because he was never letting her go. They'd tumble through the centuries determined to claim her for their own, and rightfully so. But he'd fend them off, every one.

He should probably learn a martial art of some sort.

Finally, she stirred beneath him, and he lifted up to see a pleased, lazy smile on her gorgeous face. A new expression, and his favorite, bar none.

"Thomas?" She flicked his earlobe with a gentle forefinger. "Sometimes your single-minded concentration is a really, really good thing."

When he laughed, she laughed too, and he had to discover how that tasted on her lips. And then how the rest of her tasted.

Good thing they had three more days in a hotel.

He intended to spend every single moment of them in her arms.

EPILOGUE

THE TIMER CLIPPED TO THOMAS'S POCKET WENT off, and he silenced the beeping. Then he looked up from the microfilm machine in search of Callie.

They hadn't worked together as much this past year. At least twice a week, though, the two of them made sure to ask for the same shifts, and Bridget had proven accommodating. In part because she knew that Thomas, despite his best efforts, still paid more attention to his beloved fiancée than any of his other colleagues.

Callie was standing behind the desk, pinned there by a line of four harried-looking historical interpreters, their buckled shoes tapping. Her gaze caught his, and she nodded.

He turned to his patron. "I'll need to keep working on this later today or tomorrow. Could you give me your contact information, and I'll let you know when the copies are ready?"

Less than a minute later, he was hustling to the desk and checking out three books for a man in a navy waistcoat and rolled-up sleeves. Then helping the next woman, her ruffled neckline wrinkled in the summer heat, find books on the material history of colonial America.

When the line had disappeared, Callie smiled at him. "Thanks, babe. Can you man the desk alone for a while? I have a question that'll take some digging."

He smiled at her. "Off you go."

She squeezed his arm as she headed for the archives, and he followed her progress across the library. Hopefully that department was fully staffed today, because otherwise she might have to wait a while. Which he didn't mind, but Callie got anxious when she was gone for too long, worried that her partner on the desk might need her help.

Especially him, because multitasking still wasn't his bailiwick.

But soon, she wouldn't have to worry about covering for his continued lapses. The archives department had gladly hired him to replace their most recent retiree, so he'd be out of her gorgeous hair within a month.

At least at the library. At their apartment, there was no getting rid of him, and that was precisely what she wanted. Which he knew, because he often *asked* what she wanted— and because she'd trained herself to discuss any discontents she might have, at home or work.

A scowling patron appeared in front of the desk, tricorn hat tipped back.

"I received a notice that I have an overdue book." The man seemed to consider this a personal slight against him, entirely caused by Thomas. "But I know I returned it already, so—"

With his usual limited success, Thomas tried to eject Callie from his thoughts and get back to work. Because, as the past year's experiences had taught him, such patrons required a lot of effort. The book, in all likelihood, would not be sitting in the stacks or on the shelving carts. Tricorn Man would insist angrily that the library had lost it.

And then Tricorn Man would return it within several days, probably via the drop box.

Callie called it the Drop Box of Shame and Regret because of such occasions, as well as its exclusive use by patrons whose cats had urinated on the library's books.

As always, she was hilarious and acute. A marvel.

He couldn't wait to marry her and spend two whole, uninterrupted weeks on Renaissance Island with her, sans camera crew, for their honeymoon. But he could hold out three more months. Probably.

Half an hour later, she came bustling back to the desk, that snug suit and fancy bun making her look like the sexiest and most successful CEO on all seven continents.

He abandoned the computer monitor in favor of a better view, pushing his glasses up to the bridge of his nose. "Did you acquire several Fortune 500 companies while you were gone?"

She snorted out a giggle. "Sadly, no, despite my best efforts and most corporate attire. But I got what I needed from the archives." Her lips still curved, her brown eyes still bright with mirth, she gave him a discreet pat on the ass. "So you can get going again, babe. Thanks for the help."

He reset his timer for another ten-minute stint and returned to the microfilm machine.

And did so thinking, as he always did, that his entire conception of happiness was encompassed in one word and one image.

Callie, and that beam of a smile directed his way.

THE END

THANK YOU FOR READING *DESIRE AND THE DEEP BLUE SEA*.
♥ I hope you enjoyed Callie and Thomas's story! Please consider leaving a brief review where you got this book. Reviews help new readers figure out if a book is worth reading!

If you would like to stay in touch and hear about future new releases in this series or any of my other series, sign up for the Hussy Herald, my newsletter:

https://go.oliviadade.com/Newsletter

And turn the page for a list of my other books and a suggestion on what to read next!

ALSO BY OLIVIA DADE

LOVESTRUCK LIBRARIANS

Broken Resolutions

My Reckless Valentine

Mayday

Ready to Fall

Driven to Distraction

Hidden Hearts

THERE'S SOMETHING ABOUT MARYSBURG

Teach Me

Cover Me / Work of Heart

LOVE UNSCRIPTED

Desire and the Deep Blue Sea

Tiny House, Big Love

PREVIEW OF TINY HOUSE, BIG LOVE

PROLOGUE

Cowan paused the video footage on his monitor—small, as befitted a lowly intern at the Home and Away Television Network—and turned to Irene. "This dude's definitely a serial killer."

She glanced up from her tablet, where she'd been answering texts and messages from various HATV staff. "He looks normal enough to me."

As he'd discovered over the past weeks, her standards for applicants to Tiny House Trackers were simultaneously more and less stringent than this. When they screened submissions, she weeded out anyone she considered boring, even people he considered acceptable options. Accountants, data entry clerks, lawyers: all dismissed with a flick of her wrist.

Potential murderers, however, did not appear to constitute a problem for her.

"He was very insistent that his tiny house have large storage areas with sturdy locks on the outside and no knobs on the inside. Also room on the walls for his meat hooks." Cowan shuddered. "God help any census taker who stops by during fava bean season."

She didn't look convinced. "Maybe he hunts wild boar or sasquatches or something."

"Sasquatches don't exist."

"I'm a city girl." She shrugged. "All wildlife seems mythical and exotic to me."

"I don't think the greater ease of Sasquatch hunting is the reason he wants to live alone in the woods." He leaned forward, ready to click to the next interview. "As far as I'm concerned, he's a no."

Her stylus tapped against the edge of her tablet as she considered the matter. "Not so fast. Featuring him might help goose our ratings. Maybe we could even propose filming a follow-up special, *Tiny House of Terror.*"

She might have begun her internship with HATV only a few months before him, but that time had clearly jaded her.

"Forget it." He typed NO into his applicant spreadsheet, letting the rare all-caps refusal express his strong feelings on the matter. "I'm not going to be responsible for any tiny house carnage."

"Suit yourself." She turned back to her messages. "But don't blame me when we end up featuring yet another cash-strapped single with four enormous dogs who wants full-size appliances, a bathtub, and a king bed in less than a hundred square feet for a budget of about twenty bucks."

He cringed at the mere thought of it.

Right now, the two of them were sitting in a forgotten corner of the HATV studios, occupying a room of approximately that same size. Only a couple of chipped desks, two computers, and stained tan carpeting filled the space. Yet even without a single microwave, bathtub, or mattress, the force of Irene's presence made the room feel tight.

He couldn't imagine trying to fit an entire household into such a tiny footprint. But that's what people had been clamoring to do, and they wanted to broadcast their tiny house search via HATV. Which meant interns like he and Irene spent way too many hours sorting through applicants.

With a sigh, he clicked on the next possibility, a thirty-something woman named Lucy Finch. "Better a boring participant than someone who hunts villagers for sport."

She snorted. "After another month of this, you'll think differently. Trust me."

When Lucy Finch filled his monitor, he groaned. "Oh, Jesus. Another latter-day hippie type."

"Told you," Irene said.

He began to take stock of the woman. White. Brownish-blond hair. Brown eyes. Tortoise-shell frames for her glasses. Long, frizzy curls that tangled with her dangling peace-sign earrings. No makeup. A nose stud and a wide, tentative smile. Some kind of flowy tie-dyed top, and if he wasn't mistaken...

He looked closer, squinting as she wiggled in the chair to get herself settled.

Yup. No bra. Well, it couldn't hurt to hear her out, right?

"Tell us about yourself," urged Martha, the woman who conducted all the interviews for Tiny House Trackers. "Your name, your job, and why you need a tiny house."

"I'm Lucy Finch." The woman was fiddling with something in her palm, rubbing her thumb in circles against it again and again. "I'm a licensed and Board-Certified massage therapist in Marysburg, Virginia. I used to manage our local Massage Mania, but I was just promoted. Now I'm going to help open new locations around the country and train their managers and employees."

His eyebrows rose. It seemed Ms. Finch possessed a certain amount of ambition.

With her free hand, she tucked a hank of curls behind her ear. "I'll be moving frequently. I decided living in a tiny house that could move with me made more sense than month-by-month rentals or hotel rooms. And I liked the idea of paring my belongings down to the minimum and leaving a smaller carbon footprint."

"Why did you choose to apply to Tiny House Trackers?" Martha's warm voice came from behind the camera. "What factors played into your decision?"

The woman winced. "Well, to be honest, it wasn't really my idea. My friend Allie convinced me."

A rustling of papers offscreen. "And Allie is your real estate agent?"

"She said she could find me a great tiny house in the area. I'm not quite sure what I want yet, but—"

"A yurt." Irene was still perusing her tablet. "That type always goes for a yurt."

"You don't know that." He gestured to the monitor. "She might choose a cabin in a forest where she can hug trees whenever she wants. Or a converted train car that she'll paint with peace symbols and decorate with tie-dyed scarves and posters of Jerry Garcia. There are lots of possibilities."

"Mark my words. There are yurt people and non-yurt people, and trust me, kid, she's a yurt person."

He folded his arms across his chest. "I'm actually older than you."

"Maybe in years. Not in wisdom."

Lucy Finch was still talking. "—room to store my massage table when I'm not using it, in case I see clients on the side. A bathroom big enough for those clients to change. If I have a loft, steps instead of a ladder, so my dog can—"

Blah, blah, blah. Sweet smile and braless state notwithstanding, her story wouldn't grab viewer attention, not enough for their ratings to draw even with their competitor's tiny house show, and she didn't seem like the type to break down or throw a fit on camera. Not good fodder for unscripted television.

He made a few notes in the spreadsheet and prepared to reject yet another potential participant. Dammit, Irene had a point when it came to Mr. Silence of the Tiny House Lambs. Maybe they could conduct a poll during the episode about whether the man hunted wildlife or hapless tourists, and even add a few tips in a chyron about how to escape from backwoods cabins of horror.

Martha was wrapping up her questions. "Would you want to include a friend or significant other in your tiny house search?"

Poised to click to the next interview, his hand stilled on the mouse.

With that question, Ms. Finch's whole demeanor had changed. Her smile spread to her eyes, which crinkled appealingly behind her glasses. Her thumb slowed its circles, then stopped altogether. Her shoulders lowered, and she sat back in her chair.

"If you chose me as a participant, my friend Sebastián Castillo would accompany me." She laughed, the sound warm and low. "Much to his dismay."

"He didn't want to help you?" Martha's voice had sharpened, but not with impatience. With interest, as she sensed the same shift Cowan had.

"He likes to keep a low profile. He'd rather break a limb than be on television." She wrinkled her nose. "I felt terrible about asking him, but I need his support and input. I trust him more than anyone else I know. And when I offered to bother someone else, he said that wasn't necessary."

Beside him, Irene had raised her head to watch Ms. Finch. "Huh."

"How long have you and Sebastián known one another?" Martha asked.

"Since high school. His family moved from California to be closer to relatives in the D.C. area, and we became friends almost immediately. Even after graduation, we stayed in touch through letters and phone calls, and we saw each other whenever he came to visit his parents. When he moved back to Marysburg last year, we became close again."

She'd set aside the object in her palm, placing it on a nearby table. A rock, he now saw. A worry stone. And as she talked about Sebastián, she gestured with both hands, her face lit with enthusiasm.

"Have you two ever dated?"

"No." Ms. Finch paused, and her smile turned wistful. "No. Although I always wond—" She cut herself off. "No, we haven't."

"Would Mr. Castillo's wife or husband object to his assisting you? Or a significant other of some sort?"

Clever Martha. Cutting to the heart of the matter in the guise of professional concern.

"He's not dating anyone right now." Ms. Finch bit her lip. "He broke up with his last girlfriend shortly after I moved to Marysburg."

"I just bet he did." Irene had shoved her tablet to one side and was drumming her fingers on the desk, as she always did when excited. "Cowan, switch to his interview."

Lucy Finch's brows had drawn together. "But I don't want to give you the wrong impression. Our relationship has never been romantic in any—"

Sebastián Castillo's face replaced his longtime friend's on the monitor.

Golden-brown skin. Black hair, short along the sides, longer and a bit choppy on top. Either dark brown or black eyes. Thick brows. Clean-shaven. A crisp button-down shirt, his tie slightly loosened and askew.

Unlike Ms. Finch, he didn't bother to force a smile. He wasn't frowning, either, though. Instead, his face revealed nothing. No nervousness. No impatience. No emotion whatsoever. His expression was as smooth as Ms. Finch's worry stone.

It remained so as he answered Martha's initial question.

His hands lay flat on the table before him. "I'm thirty-three. A mechanical engineer. I help my company modify our engine designs to meet upcoming emissions legislation."

Martha didn't waste any more time on irrelevant topics. "And why did you agree to help Lucy with her tiny house search?"

Irene had leaned forward, her green eyes sharp on Mr. Castillo's face.

Cowan returned his attention to the interview just in time to see the transformation.

Sebastián Castillo's stony façade cracked at the mere mention of Lucy Finch's name. His countenance softened, his fingers curled into loose fists, and the corners of his mouth tucked inward. An abortive smile? A frown of worry? Cowan couldn't tell, but it was something. Something that might make for very, very good television.

"She needs me." That's all Mr. Castillo said. For him, that was clearly enough.

"And you'd do anything for her?" Martha prodded.

At that, an almost indecipherable smile stretched his lips, affectionate and a touch sad. "Anything. Even go on a cable reality show."

Irene whistled. "He's a handsome devil when he smiles."

Cowan let out his own slow breath as he battled irrational annoyance. "He's also half in love with Lucy Finch, unless I miss my guess."

"I think the feeling's mutual." Her head tilted, and her fingers resumed drumming against the table. "Although I suppose they could just be really good friends and nothing more."

"Maybe." With reluctance, he pointed out the obvious. "She's about to buy a yurt and move away from him."

His coworker reached for her tablet and opened a new document. "Maybe that'll depend on how the tiny house hunt goes."

He slanted her a warning look. "We can't sabotage the houses she sees."

"That's correct. But my guess is that the options are limited in her corner of Virginia." Irene's gamine face, so familiar after weeks of working side by side, stretched into a grin. "And we don't have to help her real estate agent find better ones. We can also give a heads-up to the crew."

Any certainty he'd briefly possessed was crumbling into doubt. "I'm not sure we should mess with people's lives for the sake of good TV."

"We aren't doing it for the sake of good TV. It's more of a humanitarian mission than anything else. A good deed." A gleaming swath of jet-black hair swung in front of her face, hiding her expression. "Aren't Boy Scouts like you supposed to like good deeds?"

His head gave a warning twinge, as it often did when Irene got that particular tone.

"I don't know. It still seems a bit...manipulative, I guess. And I wasn't a Boy Scout." He hesitated, then amended, "Not for long, anyway."

She snickered. "Nailed it."

"Irene..." He scrubbed his face with both hands.

"Trust me."

He didn't. But he also didn't object when she sent a quick note to their boss.

I think we have our next episode. Suggestions for the crew forthcoming.

CHAPTER ONE

Coffee. Sebastián needed coffee. Preferably in IV form, administered stat.

An entire week loomed ahead of him, full of cameras and microphones and intrusive questions and strangers and too-tight spaces. Full of Lucy and the prospect of her imminent departure.

Not since high school had he confronted such an exciting array of horrors, and he hadn't missed that tug of dread deep in his gut. It was a familiar but unwelcome companion, dragging him by the hand into shadows.

So yeah, if he didn't plan to break his promise to his best friend—and he wouldn't, although he knew she would react to his about-face with her usual easygoing acceptance—he could at least ensure he remained adequately caffeinated, despite his pre-dawn awakening and early arrival at work. Despite the entire day of—God help him—filming that awaited him.

His fellow early-bird coworkers had gathered around the employer-provided gourmet coffee machine, their version of an old-school water cooler. But he didn't have any choice in the matter. He couldn't wait them out, not this morning.

They moved aside so he could reach the machine, and their conversation—something about sacks and yardage—continued while he filled his stainless-steel mug.

Only Gwen greeted him with a nod, her silver-streaked ponytail swinging. "Morning."

She still hadn't given up on him, even after a year. Nice lady, but entirely too persistent.

"Morning." He nodded to her and swiveled toward the mini-refrigerator. Just a splash of milk, and he'd be—

"We were just talking about the game last night. Are you a football fan, Sebastián?"

At her question, all the other engineers turned to him, and he paused.

Football didn't interest him. Fútbol was more his speed. But they didn't need to know that. Maybe they'd make fun of how much foreigners loved soccer, and maybe they wouldn't.

He wasn't willing to risk it.

"Sure," he said, pouring the milk carefully into his mug.

Bill, the resident expert on all things sports-related, brightened. "Any particular team? The Rams? The Raiders?"

Sebastián never should have told them he'd moved from California, but how could he avoid a direct question without damaging his already-tenuous relationships with his colleagues? And how could he get out of this conversation with speed but without outright rudeness?

"They're all great." A quick sip from his mug established that he'd added enough milk. "Listen, I need to get going. I'm leaving work early today, and I have a few projects to complete before then. Have a good day, everyone."

A forced smile, this one directed at the whole group, before he made his escape.

One obstacle down. But compared to what lay ahead of

him, an entire day of public exposure and claustrophobic rooms and Lucy, the conversation at the water cooler was nothing. He'd need to keep a tight lid on himself. More so than usual, even.

At his desk, he put in his earbuds and started a MATLAB simulation running. And when Gwen called across the room and asked him where he was going later that day, he pretended not to hear.

———

"THIS COZY CABIN IS ONE HUNDRED AND TWENTY square feet, has one sleeping loft, and comes in ten thousand dollars below the top end of your budget." Allie gestured toward the dilapidated wooden shack nestled among the trees. "I think it's a great option for you."

Lucy pursed her lips, attempting not to laugh on camera. *Cozy* was clearly real-estate-agent code for *ridiculously small*.

Sebastián said nothing, just studied the structure in silence. Then again, Lucy hadn't expected him to express his opinion without prompting. After all these years, he was unlikely to change his communication style, whether or not cameras and a boom mic hovered nearby.

"What are your first impressions?" Allie asked.

Lucy searched for a diplomatic answer. "I love the setting. Very tranquil."

Sure, she wouldn't actually live in this area much longer, and the house didn't come with the property. But maybe viewers wouldn't remember that.

"You won't leave much of a carbon footprint with this option." Allie's smile seemed brighter than normal. Wider too. "And what an opportunity to make this place your own with a few minor updates!"

More code. By *a few minor updates*, Lucy assumed Allie

meant *extensive renovations to keep your flimsy new home from collapsing under the weight of an errant chipmunk.*

Allie rapped on a piece of dry, cracked siding with her knuckles. Then, when it creaked ominously at the contact, she snatched her hand away. "And just look at the lovely natural patina of this wood."

Ah, yes. Patina. Also known as dry rot.

Ostensibly, Allie was talking to her, but Lucy's friend and real estate agent kept one eye on the camera at all times. She was also sporting a sleek bob, instead of her normal mop of curls. New highlights, too, along with a sharp suit.

During each break in filming, she didn't hang out with Lucy and Sebastián. Not even to tell them one of her notoriously dirty jokes or share recent pictures of her kids. Instead, she kept pumping the crew for information and dropping tidbits from her own résumé.

For years, Allie had talked about leaving what she considered the stifling confines of Marysburg, not to mention the orbit of her feckless ex-husband. Lucy just hadn't realized the search for a tiny house was meant to serve as her friend's exit plan. She should have, though, when Allie had pushed her to apply for Tiny House Trackers.

And really, why shouldn't Allie grasp this opportunity? Her friend deserved the future of her dreams, after all. If Lucy had hoped for a bit more support during this process, that was a problem with her, not Allie. This was, it seemed, yet another occasion in which Jarrod's complaints about Lucy's naïveté had proven correct.

Even two months after their breakup, she could still hear his voice. His disdain.

She slipped her hand into the pocket of her skirt. Her worry stone—amethyst for calm—slid into her palm, a welcome and familiar weight. She rubbed her thumb against the smooth, cool surface as she contemplated her first tiny house possibility.

She turned to Sebastián. "What do you think?"

"What I think isn't important." He stepped closer to her, his black hair shining almost blue in the dappled forest sunlight. "This experience is all about you. So what are your first impressions?"

She bit her lip. "I'd hoped it would be a bit bigger."

At least two hundred square feet, as she'd told Allie. Big enough for Hairy Garcia, her energetic golden retriever. Big enough to have room for her massage table.

"Well, you wanted a tiny house!" Allie laughed, but her eyes flashed a warning. "You need to be realistic, Lucy."

A comment she'd heard before, too many times. Lucy studied the leaves underfoot, her thumb circling and circling.

"I believe she asked for at least two hundred square feet." Sebastián widened his stance, his right eyebrow cocked. "This is significantly smaller than that."

Her shoulders unknotted, and she let out a slow breath of relief. Yes. Yes, that was exactly what she'd have said to Allie, if only she were capable of it.

Ever since Sebastián had transferred to Marysburg High as a junior, he'd always defended her from anything that might hurt her, even while he'd fended off countless bullies of his own. Too many of their classmates had proven eager to hassle the new kid in school, a Guatemalan-American boy who hadn't grown tall or strong until well after graduation. A boy who refused to cower or back down no matter what was said or done to him. A boy who gradually shut off all visible emotional reactions to make himself an unsatisfying target for his persecutors.

A boy who became her best and most faithful friend.

Her battles, her wounds, had not been nearly as vicious or

bloody as his. Still, he'd tried to protect her to the best of his ability. He might not have ever expressed his affection for her in words—she suspected he might not even be *able* to do so, not anymore—but he'd demonstrated that affection so many times she couldn't doubt it.

Behind a fold of her skirts, where the camera couldn't see the gesture, she took his hand in hers. It was broad and warm and strong now, vital and electric. A man's hand, not a boy's. But it was still the hand of the best champion an easily hurt teenage girl could have had. She gave his fingers a squeeze of gratitude, and then let him go, before someone could draw the wrong conclusion about them.

Someone like her, for example.

She'd always thought that someday, maybe…

But it wasn't going to happen. Not now, as she prepared to move halfway across the country. No matter how enticing he appeared in that formfitting Henley and those well-worn jeans. No matter how soft and warm his eyes became when he looked at her. No matter how her fingers tingled when they touched.

The camerawoman moved closer to Allie, capturing her tight smile in response to Sebastián's matter-of-fact challenge.

"Yes, Lucy wanted a slightly bigger house. But the supply of tiny houses in this area of Virginia is limited, as you know. That said, I'm sure we'll find a great option among the choices I've located. Lucy just needs to be flexible." Allie headed for the door, which rose high above the forest floor because of the trailer beneath the house. "Let's go inside."

Lucy let Allie and the crew precede her. Sebastián stayed by her side, as she'd anticipated.

Unsure of the boom mic's range, she spoke in a whisper. "I'm concerned about the condition of the house. It seems more weathered than I'd hoped. And I think it's too small for my needs. Although the inside could be very charming." She paused. "In a hobbit-enthusiast sort of way. I hadn't pictured living on the wrong side of the tracks in the Shire."

He closed his eyes and bowed his head, the telltale sign he was fighting a smile.

"Come on. Spill it." She poked his arm with her free hand, startled as always by the feel of firm muscle beneath her fingertip. The foreign, enticing hardness made her want to linger, to slide her fingertips up over his shoulders and down that straight, strong back of his. Instead, she dropped her hand to her side. "Tell me what you're thinking."

When he raised his face, a small smile had cracked his stoic features. "I wonder whether the price includes cookie-making elves."

She giggled and deposited the worry stone back in her pocket. "I'm pretty sure Allie would have mentioned that."

"Because this place should include a tiny elven fudge-filled-cookie factory, given the asking price and the condition." Arms akimbo, he stared up at the cabin, his grin fading. "If it doesn't, I'd hesitate before buying."

"At least it's towable, once I get a truck." She peered at the trailer beneath the house. "Since it's approximately the size of my childhood dollhouse."

A shallow furrow in his brow appeared for a split second. "Before we go inside, I should know a little more about what you want. Just how soon do you need a house? How far will you have to tow it? And how often do you think you'll move?"

"I'm taking a few weeks of vacation to travel around the country before my new job starts, so I have a little time, but not much. And I might move...I don't know. Twice a year, maybe?" She hadn't asked for many details before accepting the job. The gut-level imperative to escape had driven the decision, as well as her hope that a fresh start would silence the critical voices Jarrod had left in her head. "My first assignment is in Minneapolis, but they can send me anywhere across the country."

He fell silent for a minute before responding, his voice neutral. "That's a long way."

It felt longer as each day passed and her departure from her hometown, from her clients, from her circle of female friends, and—most of all—from Sebastián became imminent.

"Don't worry." She forced a smile. "I'll write you a couple times a week, just like I always did. Maybe this time you'll do the same."

He shifted his shoulders. "I always responded to your messages."

"You did." She inclined her head. "With admirable promptness."

But he'd never initiated contact himself. Instead, he'd let her take the lead, just as he'd done since high school. If she ever stopped writing or calling him, stopped asking him to her house or inviting herself to his, she suspected she'd never hear from him again.

He wasn't capable of more, which was part of the reason she'd never pursued more from him. But what he gave her was more than enough to make him a treasured friend. One she'd miss terribly when she left Marysburg.

She knew she was important to him, even though he'd never said it.

Except maybe once, in that graduation limerick.

"Depending on where you're assigned, you might end up in vastly different climates," he said. "You'll need something sturdy, with good heating, cooling, and weather-proofing."

"And this Smurf mansion isn't it."

"Is that what you think?"

He wouldn't make the decision for her, which was both frustrating and flattering. He trusted her judgment. Now she needed to do the same.

She nodded. "Yes. Although I'm happy to tour the inside of the place for the sake of good TV, if nothing else."

As if on cue, the producer poked her head out of the cabin door. Jill didn't appear impatient, though. Instead, she grinned at the two of them with seemingly genuine warmth. "Come on up, slowpokes. And try not to speak outside of the range of the mic, if possible. We want as much usable footage as we can get."

The producer had already explained that as a relatively new and low-budget show, Tiny House Trackers used a small crew, so Lucy needed to make an effort to stay near the two cameras and the mic. And unlike a few other shows on the network, there was no script. HATV was attempting to keep the television experience authentic. So Lucy truly hadn't seen any of the houses before, much less bought one already.

She could pick one of the houses in the end, or she could choose to keep looking. From what she'd seen from Allie so far, though, Lucy suspected the latter choice would cost her a friend. And although she had plenty of those, including several true sisters of her heart, she hated to alienate anyone.

Especially Allie, her childhood neighbor. The girl who'd told scary stories in front of backyard campfires and inside tents, a flashlight beneath her chin as she wailed like a ghost. The girl who'd insisted on playing Light as a Feather, Stiff as a Board during every sleepover and always spread her sleeping bag beside Lucy's. The girl who'd been part of every birthday celebration, every block party, and every camping trip Lucy's parents had planned.

The last traces of that girl had disappeared years ago,

around the time of Allie's divorce, and Lucy understood why. But she'd always hoped the friend she'd once known might return to her someday.

Lucy was beginning to suspect that wouldn't happen. But it didn't matter, not now. Not when Allie, a camera crew, and Sebastián were all waiting for her to tour the inside of a dilapidated shack and pronounce it fit for human—or elven —habitation.

"I guess I can't put it off any longer," she muttered. "But where are my glasses?"

Sebastián produced them from his pocket. "You left them on the craft services table. You took them off to read the ingredient lists."

"Well, that explains why the house seemed kind of fuzzy, as well as tiny." She accepted the glasses and settled them on her nose. "Never mind. The house *is* fuzzy."

"Moss and mold."

She sighed. "Moss and mold on the places that don't have dry rot instead. Lovely."

"Speaking of which…" Sebastián's features had settled back into inscrutability. "Be careful on the steps."

A flimsy set of mildewing plastic steps stood before the cabin entrance. Sebastián ignored them, bounding up into the doorway with a single, athletic leap. But since she was wearing a long, full skirt, rather than pants, and couldn't boast his six feet of height, those gray-tinged steps would have to suffice for her.

He held her arm as she climbed them, not leaving the doorway until she stood on solid ground once more. Then, in unison, they shifted to look at the inside of the cabin.

No. No, no, no, no.

The words emerged before Lucy could bite her tongue. "Holy shit."

"Cut," called Jill.

TINY HOUSE, BIG LOVE IS COMING SOON! FOR RELEASE date news and preorder links, sign up for my newsletter, the Hussy Herald:

https://go.oliviadade.com/Newsletter

ABOUT OLIVIA

While I was growing up, my mother kept a stack of books hidden in her closet. She told me I couldn't read them. So, naturally, whenever she left me alone for any length of time, I took them out and flipped through them. Those books raised quite a few questions in my prepubescent brain. Namely: 1) Why were there so many pirates? 2) Where did all the throbbing come from? 3) What was a "manhood"? 4) And why did the hero and heroine seem overcome by images of waves and fireworks every few pages, especially after an episode of mysterious throbbing in the hero's manhood?

Thirty or so years later, I have a few answers. 1) Because my mom apparently fancied pirates at that time. Now she hoards romances involving cowboys and babies. If a book cover features a shirtless man in a Stetson cradling an infant, her ovaries basically explode and her credit card emerges. 2) His manhood. Also, her womanhood. 3) It's his "hard length," sometimes compared in terms of rigidity to iron. 4) Because explaining how an orgasm feels can prove difficult. Or maybe the couples all had sex on New Year's Eve at Cancun.

During those thirty years, I accomplished a few things. I graduated from Wake Forest University and earned my M.A. in American History from the University of Wisconsin-Madison. I worked at a variety of jobs that required me to bury my bawdiness and potty mouth under a demure exterior:

costumed interpreter at Colonial Williamsburg, high school teacher, and librarian. But I always, always read romances. Funny, filthy, sweet—it didn't matter. I loved them all.

Now I'm writing my own romances with the encouragement of my husband and daughter. I have my own stack of books in my closet that I'd rather my daughter not read, at least not for a few years. I can swear whenever I want, except around said daughter. And I get to spend all day writing about love and iron-hard lengths.

So thank you, Mom, for perving so hard on pirates during my childhood. I owe you.

If you want to find me online, here's where to go!

Website: https://oliviadade.com
Newsletter: https://go.oliviadade.com/Newsletter

facebook.com/OliviaDade

twitter.com/OliviaWrites

goodreads.com/OliviaDade

ACKNOWLEDGMENTS

Whenever I send a story to Mia Sosa, Kate Clayborn, and Emma Barry, I know their feedback will improve my writing immensely, even when I don't want to hear it. Maybe *especially* when I don't want to hear it. :-) Thank you for helping my books shine, without fail.

Also, without the assistance of Cecilia Grant, Sionna Fox, Susannah Nix, Zoe York, and Lori Carter, this story would still be on my hard drive. Thank you for helping me inflict it upon an unsuspecting world.

Therese Beharrie has been a loving friend and supporter as I've struggled these past few months, and I don't know how I would have kept going without my beloved alpha billionaire boss. ♥

To my family: Thank you for loving me in a way I can't doubt, despite my best efforts. I love you too, always.

CPSIA information can be obtained
at www.ICGtesting.com
Printed in the USA
LVHW041412020619
619874LV00003B/552/P